LOCK THE DOORS

Damian Myron

Myron, Damian. Lock the Doors

1

Bobby paddled furiously toward the shore, muttering repeatedly that Pop would not be pleased. The fish hadn't even teased him with a nibble, and if the alarm on his watch hadn't gone off, he didn't doubt he'd still be napping on the lake.

By the time he reached the shore, the day had ripened well into the evening, and all the chores he'd forgone in favor of fishing would have to wait until tomorrow. As he rebuked himself for his laziness, he found his voice growing as harsh as Pop's, and counted himself lucky that the old man wasn't around to administer one of his lashings.

Any thoughts of punishment would have to wait. His alarm went off again, reminding him he was late treating his condition.

Bobby grew crankier seeing his neighbor, Mr. Harris, driving along the shores. Residents along the lake were told not to drive across the shorelines because it would erode the already-thin coast, but Mr. Harris did it anyway, because driving along the winding road was inconvenient.

His patience was tested further still when Mr. Harris stopped to chat, telling him he was taking off for the weekend. In that regard, Bobby couldn't blame him. The Boyle brothers had started their Memorial Day celebration even earlier than last year, not even waiting until Friday to set off their fireworks. Bobby was glad to know he wasn't the only one who hated trying to fall asleep while it sounded like there was a shooting gallery outside.

Not picking up on Bobby's desire to leave, Mr. Harris asked how his latest fishing excursion had gone. Bobby believed the question was a veiled jab at him as the man could plainly see he had come back empty-handed, and replied he had a whopper on the line that just got away.

Mr. Harris's smirk suggested he'd caught Bobby napping, but Bobby refused to back down from the statement. The rest of his replies to Mr. Harris's interrogation were curt until his neighbor finally took the hint and drove off.

He noticed some of the tools he'd left strewn about the backyard along the path back up the hill to his house, when he'd opted to play instead of work. The sun was already setting, which was only going to make it harder to find where he'd littered Pop's tools.

And Pop wouldn't like knowing that I'd left them out overnight, Bobby thought.

"WHAT ARE YOU DOING?"

Bobby may have towered over most people in town, but when he heard the question, he felt he could hide behind a blade of grass. The voice sounded just like Pop's when he used to bark orders at Bobby.

But it can't be Pop. You buried him three years ago.

He stared ahead to his house. A van he'd never seen was parked in the cracked semicircle of pavement that was his driveway. Someone had turned on the lights in his house.

They're already inside!

2

Bobby scurried up the trail to his house, sprinting between trees, trying to limit his exposure from the windows.

The same voice boomed, "I asked you a question!"

The question reinforced one thing: They sounded hostile.

"Hmm?" a calmer, almost dreamy voice answered the angry one, as Bobby crouched behind the closest tree to the cabin he called home.

"I asked what the *fuck* are you doing?" the angry voice demanded. It was so loud the pane of glass couldn't even muffle it.

Bobby could peer inside from his hiding spot and count how many intruders had invaded his home. If he dared to peek around the trunk. Which he didn't. Two different voices were disturbing, but the appearance of the van suggested there were more. The voices were coming from his living room, which made up half the house, and also had plenty of windows to look out of.

"Oh, just checking out some of the antique guns in this case," the calm, collected voice replied. This voice was softer as it passed through the closed window, but still spoke loud enough for Bobby to hear the words just fine.

Bobby's stomach wrenched itself in a knot so violently he almost vomited. His body began to quiver over the thought that they were now armed. He hugged himself close to the tree. He didn't like the idea of being seen. Not by this lot.

Bobby pictured the room. Pop had designed it to be the grandest room in the cabin. It was the first room guests saw when walking through the front door, and though the cabin had two floors, Pop hadn't built any rooms above it, making the entire space two stories tall. The bedrooms were all built above the kitchen, laundry room, pantry, and a bathroom that made up the other half of the first floor.

Pop had built a staircase leading up to the top floor in the middle of the house where the living room met the rest of the rooms that were crammed into the remaining half of the house. A door leading to some stairs that went down into the cellar had been built under this staircase so the empty unused space didn't detract from the magnificence of the living room.

He'd left a gap between the bedrooms and where the staircase finished its ascent to the top floor. Pop had explained to Bobby that this way, guests on the bottom floor could look up and see that the room had what looked like a balcony overseeing them, and guests on the top floor could look down from their perch and behold the grandeur of the room from another angle.

Bobby could've gone on and on, but reminded himself his mind was wandering and he needed to focus.

If they were admiring Pop's rifles, they were probably standing in front of his gun case, which, when entering the front door, was tucked in the near right corner of the living room. Bobby was hiding along the side of the house where Pop had built the hearthstone of the fireplace, which when entering the front door was in the near left corner when you came through the front door, and with all the living room furniture huddled around and facing it. Before he could chastise himself for letting his mind wander again, he heard the van door slam shut. Bobby could see there was nothing blocking his view of the van.

Which meant *he* could be seen from the van.

3

He moved less than a statue. Bobby only saw the third member of the party when he walked into his line of sight, taken aback that he looked as hulking in size as Bobby did. To his relief, this new intruder was hauling a large duffel bag over his shoulder, which blocked his view of Bobby.

"That's the last of it," a deep voice called to the intruders inside, and Bobby was surprised again, this time by the fact he was tracking a woman.

He finally allowed himself to breathe when she disappeared inside. Bobby massaged his chest, repeating the mantra that she hadn't seen him.

"I told you I'd help, Regina," the calm voice said.

"I don't mind," she said, her words followed by a heavy thud.

What the hell did she have packed in that bag? Bobby asked himself.

"It kind of reminded me of my weight-lifting competitions," she said fondly. "I miss those the most."

"Let's get started already," another voice insisted, this one smug and bored.

There's four of them!

"Not yet," the rage-filled voice of the hothead snapped. "Antique guns, huh?"

Bobby guessed he was addressing the owner of the calm voice who had discovered Pop's collection.

"Oh, yeah, Brady, this is a really valuable collection here," the calm, collected voice responded. "I've hunted with my old man since I was eight, and we've tried out many different rifles over the years, but I've only seen most of these in magazines."

"Really rare?" Brady asked.

"Some of the rarest."

"Are they worth a lot, Decker?" the smug voice asked, no longer sounding bored, and a little too interested for Bobby's liking.

"I know a couple collectors, Wesley, who'd pay handsomely to get their hands on one of these. That one there"—the one called Decker paused, and Bobby imagined them pointing to one of Pop's rifles still in the case— "has one of the longest ranges for a rifle. That one"—he paused again to showcase another— "has got the softest kickback when firing.

"And this one," Decker paused once more, and this time, Bobby envisioned him talking about the gun he was holding, "has a reputation for never jamming, if it's properly maintained."

Bobby shifted back and forth uneasily on his feet. It was creepy the way Decker sounded honored just to be in the same room with Pop's guns, let alone holding them.

This is what happens when I don't lock the doors, Bobby thought.

Well, why would you? Who comes down here, anyway?

Inside, Decker continued, still enthralled with the rifle. "There was one time my old man and I were hunting a bear. My old man had put one in its shoulder and we tracked its blood trail for almost two hours. Somehow it charged us from behind, and my rifle jammed. Could've used something as badass as this."

Mr. Harris comes down here, Bobby continued the argument with himself.

He's a businessman from the city. You remember the first time he vacationed down here? Said he loved the look of our house and asked Pop for a quote to build one just like his. Pop quoted him a ridiculous premium, and Mr. Harris didn't even bat an eye. It was just money to him. He doesn't care about any of our possessions.

"Did you *have* to kill it?" a voice asked so softly, he barely heard it through the closed window.

Bobby's heart spiked to the moon when the voice spoke, confirming there were five of them.

"Well, Kerry, we were the only ones hunting in the area that weekend, and we were worried about any repercussions if the authorities found a bear with a slug in it." Decker chuckled. "Let's just say we didn't exactly have a permit to hunt that bear."

This Decker is unashamed talking about illegal activities? Bobby asked himself.

Start working that useless gray lump in your head! These intruders let themselves into your house while you were away, and are talking about the price Pop's guns would fetch.

Bobby's mouth stood agape as he stared through the window at the intruders. He started to tell himself that they couldn't be there to rob him, but Brady interrupted his train of thought.

"If they're that valuable, you better not damage them before we leave, or I'll break your fucking neck."

Bobby nearly yelped. If Brady was willing to do that to one of his own, Bobby didn't want to think about what the hothead would do to someone he didn't know. Someone who saw things they weren't supposed to.

Hey, he finally gets it! Now will you do the sensible thing and get help?

Leaving sounded good to Bobby. He retreated back a step and tripped over the fishing pole he hadn't realized he'd set down. He nearly stepped on a hatchet lying on the ground, and recalled that he'd started off the morning hacking off slim branches from the trees before deciding it would be smarter just to cut some of them down. His chainsaw and pickaxe rested on a stump, which he'd abandoned digging up in the backyard when it had gotten too grueling. From there, he'd set a coffee can filled with nails on his cellar door and got to work repairing the exterior shutters of his kitchen until the sight of his refrigerator convinced him fishing would be a worthy excuse for a break.

Bobby groaned, visualizing all Pop's tools he'd have to collect around the house. He supposed under normal circumstances, it was good his alarm interrupted his nap, because at least he'd have some daylight left to pick them up after taking his pills.

But because Pop said I was prone to forgetfulness, Bobby thought, I programmed more than one—

Bobby's hand scrambled to his watch in a desperate attempt to keep it from—

BEEPBEEPBEEP

4

"What was that?" Kerry asked as Bobby cut off the alarm and hugged himself close to the tree.

"Probably just some bird out there," Regina replied. "Or some other woodland critter. This place is probably swarming with them. You saw how much roadkill we passed getting here, and they were still darting out in front of us."

"Maybe we should've done *our* part and added to the carcasses," Wesley's arrogant voice added.

"It didn't *sound* like some animal," Kerry replied, sounding almost apologetic for disagreeing.

Bobby found he could breathe easy again, though he still held the tree like a security blanket. He assured himself if they were suspicious of his alarm or had seen him, they would've investigated.

"*Bra-DY!*" a new, spoiled voice whined. "This place has, like, *no* cell reception."

There's a sixth!

"Perfect, Misty," Brady responded, sounding at ease for the first time. "Nothing to distract us this weekend."

"I don't like being isolated from the world like this," Kerry protested.

"There's a landline." Wesley scoffed at the antique form of communication.

There's one in the living room, and there's one in Pop's office upstairs.

The thought of the phone gave Bobby an idea. He craned his neck to his bedroom window on the second floor. Pop's office was in the room next to his. All he had to do was call the sheriff's department and hang up. Bobby wouldn't even have to risk them hearing him speak. Just a call would get a deputy to pay them a visit. As soon as he saw their car pull into his driveway, he'd emerge from his hiding spot and tell them everything. That'd take care of the intruders.

He used to sneak out of his room and shimmy down the very tree he was using as a shield from the intruders. It had been years since he'd put his stealth skills to the test, but Pop had never woken up when he went on his nightly excursions to the lake, and that was enough to convince him he could crawl inside without attracting their attention.

"Still," Kerry persisted, "being here creeps me out."

But what about my pills? I need them, he thought.

"Would you remember what we came here to do?" Brady demanded, the barely contained rage returning to his voice. "*RELAX*!"

Bobby quickly thought up a new plan. His medication was in the upstairs bathroom, right next to Pop's office. He could take his pill first, *then* call the sheriff, then escape down the tree. If he heard one of them coming up the stairs, there was always Pop's room across from the bathroom he could hide in. There was also another tree that could be reached from the two guest bedrooms opposite his room and Pop's old office. He had never tried climbing down that one, but it looked thick and strong enough to support his bulky weight.

As far as he could tell, there were only six of them, and they were all congregated in the living room. It would've been better if they'd discovered the door along the staircase that led into the cellar because that would put two floors of separation between him and them. He reckoned as long as they weren't in the kitchen or downstairs bathroom, which were directly below the rooms upstairs, they weren't likely to hear him once he got inside.

Bobby started to hoist himself up onto the lowest branch. He had scaled this tree enough times to master getting up and down it while using the trunk to shield himself from any prying eyes inside.

The living room window he'd been listening through popped open. Bobby froze in place, mostly suspended in the air. Only the tip of his toe still balanced on the ground. His arms were screaming at him to let go, but he didn't dare. They were sure to hear him drop.

But they're going to see your fingers holding the branches!

To his horror, more than his fingers were exposed to the intruders. He could peek past the trunk in through the open window, making the top of his head visible to anyone looking outside.

All he could bring himself to do was hang there and pray no one noticed him. A slender arm emerged from the window, swinging a cell phone. He stifled a gasp each time the hand came close to the tree, fearing whoever was attached to the phone would take notice of him hiding behind it.

"No reception *here*, either," Misty's whiny voice pouted before Bobby heard footsteps receding from the window.

Finally, a girl ignoring you pays off.

Bobby lowered himself back to the ground, giving his arms a quick reprieve. He still intended to get inside.

"I'm going to look around," Misty announced over the other conversations taking place. "See what else this place has. Wesley, open all the windows, air this place out a little."

"Me, too," Kerry said pointedly.

Bobby groaned as he heard forceful footsteps ascending the staircase. He glanced up at his windows. If the intruders spread out upstairs, that point of entry might as well have been on Mars.

They're wasting no time fanning out. They'll comb every square inch and pick the place clean.

"Kerry!" Brady called out to her. The stomping cut out, and for a moment, Bobby saw he still had an opening to climb inside. Then his ears picked up the familiar creak of the stairs, and puzzled out that Misty was now upstairs.

"Don't be—"

"You talked me into this, all right?" Kerry cut Brady off.

Given the way the rest of the room gasped, Bobby assumed doing this to Brady was unheard of. "You convinced me we needed to do this. So, if I'm forced to go along, give me some space, okay?"

Bobby braced himself against the tree, waiting for an eruption that never came. Kerry continued up the stairs, and Brady waited until she was out of earshot to start grumbling that she was a moody bitch. The only sound he heard coming from the bottom floor was the rest of the windows being opened. The rest of the intruders remained mute, and Bobby didn't blame them. It didn't sit well listening to Brady trash a girl like that, but Bobby didn't want to be on the receiving end of that wrath.

Above him, his bedroom door closed. The thought of one of them in his room chilled him. He had always fantasized about a girl in his bedroom, but not under these circumstances.

"Last thing I need is for her to ruin the big plans I've got for us this weekend," Brady continued to mutter inside.

Bobby studied the branches above him. The tree shed its leaves as soon as autumn struck, but being on the cusp of summer, he felt confident he could scale the tree and remain hidden in the foliage from anyone looking out his bedroom window.

"Why don't you cool off?" Regina suggested, growing irritated by Brady's rant.

Muscle memory took over, and Bobby got balanced comfortably on the top branch in a flash. He glanced down at the living room window to see if he had alerted the intruders.

"Good idea," Brady snarled, failing to contain his frustration. "There was a place we passed about a mile from here that should have what we need. Why don't I go pick up some more supplies for this weekend?"

As far as Bobby could tell, the brute hadn't heard him. Nor had the rest of them.

Feeling safe, he turned his attention to the woman sitting on his bed. She had her back to him, but he got the impression she was doing her best to hold back sobbing. She also looked nothing like a hardened criminal.

The woman glanced at Bobby's nightstand, and picked up a framed picture of him and Pop that had resided there since Pop's passing. After getting lost inspecting it, she let out a deep sigh.

"What are you doing here, Kerry?" she asked herself.

This must be her first heist, Bobby thought. He wondered what she was doing with this crew as well. Downstairs, she'd said Brady had convinced her they needed to do this, and his mind lacked the imagination to dream up what this lost, innocent-looking girl could've gotten mixed up in that led to her falling in with this crowd.

"Anyone else need anything?" Brady asked below, though it came out as a demand. No one responded.

"*Look* at the *size* of this one!" Misty exclaimed from the other side of the house. "I've got *this* room!"

That's Pop's room!

As deftly as he'd gotten up the tree, Bobby negotiated his way back to solid ground. He wasn't sure he could call the sheriff in time to stop them, and if he couldn't, he had to know what to report missing. Bobby hadn't been in Pop's room much since he'd passed, and even before then he'd gone in sparingly. It was a mystery to him what he'd have to report stolen unless he witnessed what they found.

Bobby kept himself low to the ground as he scrambled to the other side of the house. The untamed bushes surrounding the house he had neglected to prune that morning provided the perfect cover from the strangers inside. There was a brief moment when he almost kicked over the can of nails he'd left on the cellar door, but as far as he could tell, he was up another tree before they were any the wiser.

"*I'll be right back!*" Brady called to the group inside.

The tree Bobby was perched on was planted between the two guest bedrooms on Pop's side of the house. It didn't give him a direct view into Pop's room, but the angle he spied through caught enough of the mirror on Pop's dresser to see the entire room.

Through the mirror, Bobby could see Misty fingering the antlers of the prized buck, the largest deer Pop had ever bagged hunting, that Pop had hung on the wall. She grew bored with it, and turned toward the mirror. Bobby's breath caught. She had a captivating beauty Bobby thought only existed in magazines.

He tensed, fearing she might spot him in the mirror, even though the branch he was hiding in was lush with leaves, but she was too preoccupied admiring herself to notice him.

Even a goddess like her is drawn to her own radiance.

"I'm taking a shower," she called out. "I'm tired of being a sweaty mess."

He found it peculiar she'd take the time to shower during a robbery, but didn't question it. She seemed right at home with home invasion. Bobby guessed she was experienced enough to know how not to leave any DNA at the scene of a crime.

Her back was to the mirror as she slipped her shorts down the curve of her hips. Bobby chuckled in delight. He had never had women lining up to take their clothes off in front of him, and definitely not women who could fill his head with lustful fantasies like Misty.

And the way *she's discarding her clothes . . . it's like she knows you're spying on her, and putting on a show for you.*

But she doesn't know.

That guilt stabbed at his conscience. He pried his eyes from the window. As much as he tried to justify the continued peeping, Misty wasn't performing a striptease for him.

Bobby glanced down, searching for the best way to climb down from the tree, and froze. Waiting for him below was a man with eyes so filled with rage that he could only be Brady.

"Get a good look?"

5

Brady's hands were like vise grips as they yanked Bobby's ankles off the branch. Bobby's chin smashed into the branch as he fell. He tasted blood immediately.

His fall was cushioned by Brady's body. The brute let out a muffled grunt as he was bowled over. Bobby scrambled to his feet, and tried to flee. His mind was so frantic it took him a second to process that he was running downhill toward the lake.

"Misty," Regina called from inside. "Before you shower, where did you put—?"

Bobby didn't catch the rest as Brady caught him in his dominant grasp again. The force of the tug on his shoulder ripped Bobby from his feet. Brady was on him the moment he crashed to the ground.

"What'd you see? Huh? What'd you see, motherfucker?"

I warned you they'd be hostile if they caught someone spying on what they were doing.

Bobby threw his arms up, shielding himself as best he could. Brady kept repeating himself, but never waited for a reply.

He was too busy raining a hailstorm of fists down on Bobby.

Brady's weight lifted off Bobby and he lowered his guard to see what was going on. He wormed away from his attacker, but was unable to avoid the sharp kick to his side.

The next kick connected with his ribs. The third folded him in two. Bobby started to roll away before Brady could launch a fourth. The strike had grazed his shoulder, and the impact was enough to accelerate his slide downhill. Brady lost his balance and fell on top of him.

The two of them tumbled down the slope together until they crashed into the stump Bobby had been digging up with the pickaxe and chainsaw.

Brady tried to brace himself for the impact, fracturing his wrist for his trouble. He would've cried out if Bobby hadn't crashed into him a moment later, causing Brady to substitute an agonized wail with a muted grunt.

Bobby rolled over the top of Brady and the stump, missing the chainsaw but dislodging the pickaxe, and continued his descent toward the lake. Roots scraped his body as he rolled over them. He landed with a thud when he mercifully reached the shore.

A tumbling accelerated down on him. The pickaxe cartwheeled toward him, and he rolled to the side moments before the spike drove itself into the ground where his neck had been.

His ears caught something else bounding down the slope, and turned to see the maniac was still in full pursuit. He didn't know where the lunatic got the energy to run after their descent.

Bobby stumbled to his feet as Brady yanked the pickaxe from the ground and chased after him.

Brady clutched his fractured wrist close to his body, but with Bobby in his sights, he was undeterred by the pain. He overtook his prey in no time, cornering him along the shoreline.

The hothead swung the pickaxe wildly, planting it in the ground.

The madman abandoned his weapon, lunging at Bobby, bowling him over into the lake. Bobby splashed around as he came up for air. His lungs filled with water as Brady was on him again, shoving his head back into the lake.

Bobby struggled to free himself from Brady's control, but no matter how many times he struck the hothead's arm, Brady's dominant grasp yielded nothing.

He couldn't hold his breath any longer. The lake poured down his airway. His pounding on Brady's arm grew less impactful as his limbs began to tire. The water muted his screams for mercy. He knew there was none for him. Brady's face held nothing but malice. It reminded him of Pop, and the similarity triggered something unexpected.

For the first time in years, he could hear Pop calling him a crybaby.

Pop's term echoing in his head still made him shudder. Pop had always ridden Bobby hard about his unwillingness to exert himself, but started calling him that and never let up when their water heater burst and flooded the cellar. He'd gotten tired of berating Bobby, demanding to know what good all those muscles were if he couldn't get through an hour of chores without complaining about being damp and whining for a break. Pop had told him whether he wanted to or not, they had to get everything out of the water before there was permanent damage, and that he better get used to life pelting him with these situations.

There were two types of people in the world, he'd told Bobby. Those who break down and cry for their mommies when things got tough, and those who steel themselves up and try. To Pop, crybabies were a dime a dozen, always bemoaning any setback, like life had it out for them. Something else was always to blame. Nature. The man. The system. Politicians. God. But *try*babies, they were special. Whether they were tired, scared, what have you, they always buckled down and gave maximum effort. And when that happened, the things they tried started getting done, and they became that *exceptional* breed called *do*babies. Anytime Pop caught Bobby slacking, his question was always the same: "Are you a crybaby or a trybaby?"

Summoning what was left of his strength, he pounded at Brady again. Bobby couldn't even lift his arms high enough to strike the maniac's arm. His fist flailed softly at the hothead's chest. It had as much impact as a fly striking concrete. He swung again, connecting with Brady's abdomen. No effect. Bobby mustered up one more swing.

And felt the maniac flinch.

He chopped both of his hands down on Brady's fractured wrist. It wasn't much. But it was enough.

Even hushed by the water, he heard Brady cry.

Bobby burst from the water with an effort that would've made Pop proud. He grabbed hold of Brady's shoulders, shoving the hothead off him and driving his foe to the ground.

Brady gasped softly, and squeezed Bobby's arm.

Bobby's lungs expelled most of the water he'd swallowed. Brady was still holding his arm, and Bobby wrenched it free. The force of his tug pulled Brady onto his stomach, and seeing this, Bobby crawled away in a panic, expecting Brady to recover quickly and strike again.

He braced himself for an impact that never came.

Bobby threw up some more water, then cast a glance back at his attacker. Brady lay face down in the lake. His flailing arms did nothing to keep him from drowning.

The blade of the pickaxe was buried deep in his back.

6

Let him drown. He was ready to kill you.

No! Bobby screamed to himself. I'm no murderer.

Bobby's mind may have wasted no time trying to save Brady, but his body didn't follow. He retched up more lake water, this time noticing a tint of red in the puddle. Now that the adrenaline of fighting for his own survival had worn off, his body was feeling the effects of falling down the hillside and Brady's thrashing.

By the time he reached Brady, the hothead was barely moving. Even Brady's gurgling was dying down. Bobby could only manage a weak tug. The body barely budged.

And then he heard the siren.

7

He snapped his head back to his house. He couldn't make out the vehicle, but the flashing lights came from his driveway. A sense of relief poured through his body. Law enforcement was here, and that meant the end of the saga with the intruders.

How did they know to come here, though? You never had the chance to get inside and call them.

Bobby fumbled coming up with an answer. While he groped for a reason why they had known to show up, Brady gave one last thrash in the water.

He gave the body jerk after violent jerk until he'd dragged Brady onto the shore. For the first time, Brady looked calm.

Dread swallowed the joy he'd felt a moment ago when he believed the cavalry had arrived. A cop was now on his doorstep for an unknown reason, and he was hunched over a dead body.

I was *defending* myself! Bobby thought. They'll see all the bruises and cuts on me and they'll believe me. They'll have to believe me.

Will they? Even after you haven't taken your pills? Go up and tell them what happened, then.

Bobby stayed rooted to the ground. It was well past when he was supposed to take his prescription. He was sure people around town knew how he got when he wasn't medicated. If he charged up there trying to explain what happened, would he make sense, or would it all come out an excited, jumbled mess?

It'll sound like another wild story from Bobby Dinwill, his inner demons tormented him.

Bobby crushed his palms to his temples, trying to silence the thought. He needed to find out why the cop had arrived in the first place. It was possible they were already there to deal with the intruders. He didn't know how, but he wouldn't question it, either. If they were, he'd rush up the hill, screaming he'd been attacked, hoping he'd make enough sense to be believed, and try to take his pill the first chance he got. Bobby didn't want to think what would happen if they weren't there to arrest the intruders.

He heard a car door open and shut on his driveway. There was only one pair of footsteps, which told him it was a sheriff's car that had pulled up. They usually rode solo. That was a good sign. The sheriff and the deputies knew him. They knew this was his house, and that he lived alone.

Bobby started to climb back up the hill, hunched over and favoring his ribs where Brady had kicked him. He wanted to get the cop's attention as soon as they saw a stranger in Bobby's house. The slow saunter of authority stopped at the sound of the front door opening.

"Is there a problem, Officer?" the snobbish voice that sounded like Wesley called out from Bobby's front door. Bobby could tell it was said with a forced smile.

Pompous ass, Bobby thought. He smiled, fantasizing about that smug grin being wiped off Wesley's face when the cuffs were being fitted to his wrists.

Just as long as it's not—

He didn't have time to finish his thought before Sheriff Knotts responded—the last voice he wanted to hear.

8

"No problem, just gettin' clumsy in my old age," Knotts replied with a sheepish chuckle. Even though it'd been years since he'd heard Knotts' voice, the sheriff still sounded like the same bumbling fool who always bungled details about everyone in town. He and Pop had laughed up a storm when Knotts extended his condolences to Mrs. Jenkins on the passing of her husband, continually reassuring her Phil was in a better place until she finally snapped "That's great for whoever that is, I just hope my beloved *Will* is doing half as well!"

"Accidentally hit the siren as I was getting outta the car," the sheriff explained.

Unbelievable. He's apologizing? To them?

Bobby trudged farther up the hill, still staying low to the ground as he approached the house, partly because of the pain in his side, partly because he wasn't sure he wanted to be seen yet, even by the sheriff. Knotts, in his usual shamble, closed the distance between himself and Wesley.

"Has anyone seen my brother?" Misty called out from the top floor. An avalanche of steps raced down the stairs. "Oh," she said, seemingly taken aback. "Hello, Officer."

"Sheriff," Knotts corrected her.

"He went out to get some more things for this weekend," Regina's husky voice explained.

Do something! Bobby's mind implored the sheriff. He knows *everyone* in town. He knows they don't belong here.

"If there's no problem, why *have* you stopped by, Officer?" Wesley asked, with the same attitude he'd given the intruders earlier. The more Wesley spoke, the more Bobby got the impression Wesley looked down on everyone who wasn't Wesley.

"*Sheriff*," Knotts corrected again. "And I stopped by because I noticed the strange van parked in the driveway."

Bobby could have let out a cheer. Knotts *did* know something was amiss. The sheriff had probably waited until he could assess the situation and see how many perps he was dealing with before letting them know he was onto them. Bobby quickened his pace up the hill, ready to volunteer as the witness Knotts needed to make arrests. He felt relieved that he'd be able to explain the body by the lake.

"That's right. *I* booked the cabin for the weekend, off of one of those websites where people rent their houses out like they're hotels," Wesley explained, taking great pride that he'd bankrolled the rental.

Knotts stood silent, contemplating what Wesley had said. For a moment, Bobby believed he was about to pick apart Wesley's lie.

"Oh, right, he told me about that."

Knotts' words brought Bobby to a dead stop. I did no such thing! Bobby roared to himself. He suddenly didn't feel safe standing out in the open, and quickly crouched behind a bush along the trail. Bobby stepped on another tool he'd left lying about, this one a screwdriver he'd misplaced a month ago, and wondered why he'd dropped it here.

Focus!

Bobby had no plans of moving from where he'd rooted himself to the ground until the conversation with Knotts played out further. Bobby still couldn't work out why he'd first arrived, and now there was this new puzzle of Knotts lying about Bobby telling him they'd be here.

What struck him the most was that Knotts didn't even sound like a cop when talking to them. He'd sounded apologetic, self-deprecating, and friendly. Bobby conceded that Knotts always spoke that way around town, but the sheriff had known the residents of the town for decades.

He's so chummy talking to the intruders, it's like they're all pals.

I need him to be more than the bumbling bozo with a badge right now, Bobby countered to himself.

"It's odd that the van is still here," Bobby heard Decker observe from the house. Even Decker's soft-spoken voice carried perfectly to Bobby's ears.

"Why's that?" Knotts asked, a slight pang of suspicion in his voice.

"Because Brady isn't. And if he didn't take off already, why didn't he come up when the siren blared?"

There was a brief pause as they contemplated it, and then Kerry offered, "You heard him raving about this place coming down here. He's probably just scoping everything out before he leaves."

The conversation informed Bobby they didn't know what had happened yet. He and Brady must've tumbled far enough down the hill they were out of earshot when the mayhem started.

"Where'd you folks say you came down from? Chicago?" Knotts asked.

"We didn't, actually," Wesley said. His tone more than suggested he wanted the sheriff to leave.

"Yes. Chicago," Regina replied. Her response was for Knotts. Her annoyed tone was for Wesley.

Chicago was the worst answer they could've given. Pop had been obsessed over the mafia, consuming countless mob movies and documentaries. A lot of those films centered around syndicates in Chicago.

"I thought I recognized your accent," Knotts said.

"Sheriff, would you like to come in?" Misty offered, her voice friendlier than it should have been.

"Don't mind if I do, darlin'."

His response was too quick. Knotts had always possessed a fascination about the cabin. When he'd first been elected sheriff, he'd paid them regular weekly visits. Pop had always told Bobby to head inside whenever Knotts came around. Bobby knew it was because Pop didn't want him hearing what was said, but Bobby always listened from his bedroom anyway.

Every visit was the same. Knotts was curious about Pop's finances. He'd speak in that friendly tone of his, posing his questions like he was asking for advice. How could Pop be retired at his age? And own a house outright? And all that land? What was his secret?

Initially, Bobby assumed Knotts had jumbled the details again. Maybe he'd gotten a tip that one of the neighbors was sitting on a stash of unclaimed income, and thought it was Pop. But even though Knotts had to be mistaken, and spoke in that same chummy manner of his, he didn't *seem* like a doofus who constantly got his facts mixed up. He seemed like the keen lawman the town had elected in the first place.

Pop refused him every time he asked to peek inside. Knotts would nod like he accepted the answer. But he'd always return.

This lasted the whole summer. Only on his last visit did he drop the friendly act. Taking on the air of authority, Knotts demanded to know how on no income Pop was able to provide for himself.

And the little retard he was raising.

To that point, Bobby had always thought Pop was overreacting when he sounded off on Sheriff Knotts. The constant bitching about unlawful searches grew old, and he always thought they'd get Knotts out of their hair if Pop just explained to Knotts that he sold Momma's old artwork from time to time.

Bobby never did, feeling Momma was still a sore subject as she was no longer with them. Pop could never bring himself to display any of her art around the cabin. He always kept her work tucked away in the crawlspace of the cellar, only retrieving one of her pieces if he was selling it.

After hearing Knotts call him that, Bobby despised the sheriff more than his old man.

Bobby wasn't the sharpest tack, but he knew he wasn't retarded. The school had performed the tests to prove it. As long as he was on his medication, he could function just fine.

Knotts' weekly poking around ended after that, maybe from embarrassment for saying that about someone's kid. The only other time Knotts had come knocking at his door was when Pop had died. Pop wasn't even in the ground a day, and Knotts had pulled up in his driveway.

The sheriff had tried to play it off as coming to offer his condolences. He wasted no time asking if Bobby was going to invite him inside. Even though Pop was gone, Knotts still suspected him of having something stashed away somewhere, something he couldn't explain having. Bobby said the one word Pop had made him promise to tell Knotts if he ever came around looking to get inside.

Warrant.

Bobby scowled as Knotts disappeared inside his house. The bastard had finally found his way in.

"Must admit, it is nice getting out of that heat," Knotts said once inside. Even though he could hear the sheriff just fine, Bobby inched closer to the house, resuming his position behind the closest tree. He wanted to see if Knotts was actually smiling now that he could poke around the house.

"I'm always happy doing anything to please law enforcement," Misty flirted.

Are they really the mafia? Bobby wondered. Brady, maybe. Regina has the size of someone who could be the muscle. The less I know about Decker, the better. But are they *really* Mafioso?

Misty didn't fit the mold of a gangster. Neither did Kerry. Bobby could wrap his head around Misty being born into a family of gangsters. Misty certainly sounded comfortable around Knotts, suggesting she'd dealt with cops in the past. He supposed Kerry could have unwittingly found out she was dating a criminal.

"I'll bet you do, darlin'," Knotts said slyly, returning her suggestive tone.

"Office—*Sheriff*," Wesley interjected. "I'm sure you can imagine we *don't* want to be *disturbed* this weekend."

Wesley spoke like someone who expected to rise to nothing less than greatness. Bobby wouldn't have been surprised if Wesley was the son of a don.

That might be why he talks down to Knotts so freely. He knows if push comes to shove, he's got Daddy as an ace up his sleeve.

"Me, neither," Knotts stated absently.

Bobby imagined Knotts hadn't pried his eyes from Misty yet. "Last thing I want is to get any sort of complaints from the residents here about this house."

If Bobby *was* dealing with the mob, they hadn't sent their best. The intruders he'd seen looked young, barely above drinking age. If Wesley was the heir apparent to the family, this may've been done so he could feel in charge. Or this could've just been a job to throw at new recruits hungry to "make their bones."

"Trust me, Sheriff. We don't want to attract any attention while we're here," Wesley insisted, his patience running thin.

"You should be more careful, then," Knotts grunted. "I can't turn a blind eye if people see what you're doing."

There was a mad scramble inside. Latches opened, and something dropped with a gentle thud, as though its landing had been heavily padded. Bobby worked out that something incriminating must've been left out in plain sight, and rather than do his job, Knotts had merely warned them to put it away. His best guess was that it'd been tools to burglarize the house.

"We'll make sure no one hears us," Wesley said quickly. For the first time, there was no trace of haughtiness in his voice. He sounded apologetic, and humble. The tone sounded bitter on his tongue.

If they've got their tools out, why isn't he arresting them? Bobby demanded to himself.

Just having the tools might not be enough. Maybe he's got to catch them in the act.

"Good," Knotts said coldly. "The residents here like the added revenue they're starting to get from tourists who've discovered this lake, but they still like to think of this place as a quiet little town where everyone knows everyone. They don't want to worry about any riffraff getting in, and I'd like to keep it that way. But if I get any complaints, I'm gonna *have* to come back here and do my job. We understand each other?"

There were murmurs of assent, followed by silence. Bobby envisioned that Knotts was taking a good long look at everything. The sheriff used to *always* do that the one summer he'd paid his weekly visits. The conversations in which he'd all but accuse Pop of hiding *something* around here would be over, but before he'd walk back to his car, he'd survey everything.

Bobby still had no idea what Knotts thought he was after, but when Knotts gave that long stare of his, Bobby always ended up praying for the sheriff to leave before he found it.

"You *really* found this place off a website?" Knotts asked.

"Yes," Kerry replied softly when no one else did. "Why?"

"Nothing. Just . . . surprised he even owns a computer."

Bobby's head perked up. For a moment, he convinced himself he'd had Knotts all wrong. He was even prepared to kiss the man.

He knows! He knows they've been lying this whole time. He's just kept up the whole friendly sheriff routine until they dropped their guard and started talking long enough for him to corner them in a lie.

Bobby didn't fight the smile carving itself onto his face. Although he lived out in the woods, he was still connected to the town's power and sewer lines. But one thing Knotts had to know was *not* connected to his house were Internet cables.

The couches groaned, and Bobby relished the thought of them shifting uneasily inside. Bobby just hoped Knotts would be able to handle all five of them if they had no plans of going quietly. He still feared they had ties to the mob.

"He must still be getting used to having one," Wesley offered. "When I was booking this place, there were barely any pictures uploaded. All of them had *terrible* resolution. When I was exchanging messages with him, it was tough to decipher what he was saying because of all the misspellings, and I had to repeatedly explain the shorthand I was using." Wesley scoffed, the superior tone returning to his voice. "The lingo I was using has been pretty standard online for *years* now."

Bobby had to hold in a laugh. He almost called out to Knotts that after all this time, he'd give his permission for the sheriff to search his house top to bottom. It'd be worth it just to hear Knotts tell the intruders there was no computer anywhere.

"Yeah," Knotts agreed. "That sounds like him. He probably went to the library or that Internet café to post this house online."

The response caught Bobby off guard. He believed Knotts had them trapped, and couldn't make out why he was letting them off the hook.

Because he wasn't trying to trap them. He was making sure they all had their stories straight in case someone spotted the van and got nosy.

No, it can't be! He's . . . he's still playing them.

What's he waiting for, then?

Bobby pressed himself for a plausible explanation and came up empty. The harsh reality set in.

Knotts *had* to be in on it.

9

Bobby ducked low to the ground as Knotts emerged from his house. The tree he hid behind shielded Knotts' view of him, and shadows created by the setting sun provided camouflage, but Bobby wasn't taking any chances of being spotted.

As far as he was concerned, Knotts was more dangerous than all the intruders combined because he had a badge.

Knotts stopped a few feet from his car. He turned to study Bobby's house, and when the sheriff's eyes swept past him, Bobby's blood ran cold, terrified Knotts had seen him.

Why's he settling for just looking at the house? Why not help them look for whatever he thinks Pop stashed inside?

Because he can't stay here. Knotts thinks you're gone for the weekend, but he's got to believe you'll file a police report. If a neighbor tells you they saw his car parked in your driveway for hours on the same day you got robbed, that'll spell trouble for him. He's got to make himself seen all around town. I'll bet he'll be writing ticket after ticket just to establish an alibi for himself.

He didn't know what Knotts expected them to find. Bobby didn't think Knotts knew about Momma's artwork. The only thing of value Bobby could think of was Momma's old jewelry, which Pop could never bring himself to get rid of. Bobby had no idea how much it was worth, if it was even worth anything. Whatever Knotts had told the mob was here, it'd been enticing enough that they'd sent people all the way from Chicago to help a small town Missouri sheriff rob a house. He supposed if they were looking to expand, having Knotts in their pocket was a start.

The thought of gangsters in his house, and Knotts' potential association, was suffocating. A small part of him still held out hope Knotts hadn't sold his soul to the mob, reminding himself that Knotts had to ask where they were from.

Bobby had watched enough gangster films with Pop to know that didn't mean anything. It was possible whoever Knotts had organized this heist with had deliberately kept the sheriff in the dark about who they were sending for this job. That way, Knotts couldn't testify against them if things went south. That Knotts was not only here, but asking questions about them, probably didn't sit well with his co-conspirators.

Knotts ended his cursory examination of the house and shambled into his car. Bobby didn't move from his spot until he could no longer hear Knotts' engine. Even with Knotts gone, Bobby didn't feel any better.

He still had no idea what to do next.

Run to a neighbor.

Mr. Harris isn't there.

So run to the next one. It might be a mile or two, but keep running until you find someone you can tell.

People will know I haven't taken my medicine.

No one knows *about that. You always wait outside Mr. Manning's pharmacy until no one's inside to pick up your refill. You always rush back home immediately so no one sees you take your pills. No one will know.*

Knotts will tell them. He'll make sure everyone knows if I accuse him of being involved in this.

There was no doubt Knotts would tarnish Bobby's name to save his own if Bobby implicated him in the robbery. He'd reveal every grisly detail he could dig up about Bobby to the public. If everyone didn't already know about Bobby's medical history, Knotts would have them all well-versed in no time.

He was also well liked as sheriff. Knotts may have been a bumbling oaf when he was first elected, but he kept crime down, kept the Boyle brothers in line (aside from their growing fireworks shows around Memorial Day and the Fourth of July), and the residents had kept him at the same post for decades now. They'd bend over backward to believe he wasn't the mastermind behind this heist.

It wasn't hard to envision how things would play out if he bolted for the nearest neighbor accusing Knotts of organizing a break-in. His story would already lack credibility if he showed up on their doorstep, drenched in sweat from running for miles, bouncing off the walls as he excitedly told a wild story implicating Knotts. That he'd been robbed would lend *some* credence to his claim, but when (not if) his condition got out, the whole town would be more than willing to sweep this incident under the rug.

Everyone would rally around Knotts. You'd likely get hauled off to the loony bin. Don't forget, there's the body you left by the lake.

I didn't kill him!

People'll believe that as much as they believe your crazy allegations about Knotts. They'll throw you in some hole and forget about you. And Knotts will have unlimited access to your house because it'll be a crime scene. He'll even be able to cut those jokers out of the score. You'll be doing him a huge favor.

Bobby balled his hands into fists. Running for help was the safest thing to do, but he couldn't leave just yet. If he had a prayer of people believing him, he'd have to appear of sound mind. Then when (not if) Knotts started telling people Bobby was "hopped up on goofballs" Bobby could at least say he hadn't stopped his regimen.

The intruders were still congregating in the living room. Bobby determined the best way inside was to climb one of the trees and sneak in through a window. His bedroom window was unlocked, but he'd have to make it down the hallway to the medicine cabinet in the bathroom and back without being seen or heard. The guest bedroom next to Pop's room was a lot closer to his target.

He believed he could be just as successful climbing into the guestroom as he was his own room. The only question was whether he'd left it unlocked as well.

"Where are you going?" Regina asked.

"To open the windows," Misty replied as footsteps clomped up the stairs. "It smells so musty and awful in here. Makes me wonder if the owner ever bathed?"

I shower!

Bobby felt Misty's deep inhales when she opened his bedroom window were a bit much. When she finished opening all the upstairs windows on his side of the house, he rounded the cabin to confirm she was opening them on Pop's side.

Footfalls came from the stairs. Bobby took it to mean Misty was vacating the top floor, allowing him a clear path to the medicine cabinet directly across the hall from Pop's room, but the rhythmic beat of soft thuds intertwined between the steps gave him pause. Misty cackled from the guestroom closest to the stairs, across from his own bedroom. Bobby realized Misty hadn't been going down, someone else had come up.

"I almost *died* at how fast you threw all your gear into your case," she said. "I wish I'd thought to take a picture of it. Not that I can post anything while we're here. Why'd you bring an attaché case anyway? Why not a duffel bag or travel case like everyone else?"

"Shut up," Wesley murmured.

"Aww, whatsamatter?" she teased him. "You worried that mean sheriff will come back and arrest you for what you've got in there?"

"He obviously hasn't returned or you'd be throwing yourself at him again," he replied dryly.

Misty huffed. "*You* obviously don't want to bunk with *me* tonight," she snapped as she stormed down the hallway.

Wesley groaned and a soft thud came from Bobby's bedroom. Bobby guessed Wesley had thrown his case in there. "Misty," he called, nearly pleading. "You know *that's* not true."

Bobby groaned as Wesley pursued her. He'd been so close to the top floor being unoccupied. A door slammed as Wesley drew near. Bobby judged the bang came from across the hall.

Great, Bobby thought. Now she's *in* the bathroom. The *one* place I need to get into.

"Misty," Wesley said, softly rapping at the door. "C'mon, open up. I didn't mean it."

He spoke barely above a whisper. Bobby had no doubt Wesley would promise Misty he'd do whatever it took to be forgiven, as long as the others didn't hear him grovel.

"Just . . . just don't degrade yourself flirting with a bum like him. He may've tried to throw his weight around down there, but it's all an act. You heard him. He's got to negotiate this town's transition into a tourist destination. But the residents, the registered voters, still want to pretend they live in this little undiscovered part of Middle America. They never want to be aware that people like us are here. The . . . . What did he call us? The 'riffraff.' As long he keeps them believing this is a quiet little town, they'll reelect him until he's ready to retire. Believe me, if he had to fill out any incident reports over this weekend, it'd be more trouble for him than for us. Just a handful of complaints will feel like a crime wave to the people of this town.

"We're out of here after this weekend, never to return. We've got lives to go back to. What'll he have?

Because they'll vote him out so fast in the next election if he can't keep the illusion going. Where's he going to go? You think any other law agency would hire someone his age?

"And that'd be the *least* of his problems if we actually *did* get in serious trouble. If he tried to press charges to save his own ass . . . well, let me just say he would *not* want to face my father in a courtroom."

There was another pause. Bobby found it insufferable waiting for a response.

So did Wesley. "What're you doing in there?" he sniped.

"Trying to find something for my headache," Misty said as the door swung open. The vacancy in her voice told Bobby she hadn't been paying attention to Wesley.

"Look at all the meds this guy takes," Misty exclaimed.

A familiar rattle twisted Bobby's stomach. At first, he tried to remain calm, assuring himself Misty had only grabbed one prescription bottle, and that it was unlikely it contained the pills he was already late taking. But then he heard a second spurt of clattering as another bottle changed hands. Then a third. Then a fourth.

By the sixth, he started to believe she'd emptied his entire cabinet.

Wesley chuckled. "I know a bunch of people who'd trade their left arm for these."

"Really?" Misty asked, for the first time expressing interest in what Wesley had to say.

"Oh, yeah. There's huge demand for these at any Ivy League school."

"Why?"

"They're desperate to keep their grades up. You've got valedictorians from Podunk little towns like this who busted their ass to get a full ride they can't afford to lose. You've got kids on student visas who dread being sent back home. This shit will keep you focused for hours, long enough to pull all-nighters. You'll crash. Hard. But after finals, who cares?"

Bobby cursed his bad luck. They had the pills he needed.

"How much would you charge them for something like this?" Misty asked. Her tone was packed with too much greed to allow any room for subtlety.

"No, you don't sell to them. You're leaving too much money on the table. You sell to those preppy assholes who need to keep off academic probation so Daddy stays happy and doesn't cut them off. *That's* where the money is."

Leaning on the tree was the only thing keeping Bobby on his feet. The intruders. The dead body on the lake. Knotts. The plot to steal his pills. Bobby may have been outside, but he felt like everything was closing in on him.

"We'd split it, right?" Misty asked, eagerly. "I found them, after all."

Wesley laughed. "Guess I'd have to give you a cut. Like a finder's fee. Would hate to have you rat me out to the rest of them downstairs."

If they take my pills . . . . But he couldn't finish the thought.

The consequences were unimaginable.

10

Whatamigoingtodowhatamigoingtodowhatamigoingto
do

Upstairs, Wesley and Misty were snickering over what they'd spend all that money on. Each coy idea Misty suggested turned into a gift for herself. Wesley not only agreed immediately with every proposal, he kept encouraging her to brainstorm, promising he'd fulfill her every desire.

It drove Bobby mad.

"All right, put those back," Wesley instructed. Misty started to protest, but he cut her off. "Where're you gonna put the bottle, hmm? You left your bag in the living room. What're they going to think if you walk downstairs with a bottle of prescribed medication that you didn't walk upstairs with? Where's Brady's mind going to jump to first?"

"*Fine*," she said, irritably.

Bobby didn't like her tone. It more than suggested she'd return for the pills the first chance she got.

He didn't know if he could get to the bottle before she could. He had to skulk in the shadows. She could move about freely. Even if he could beat her to the pills, she knew what to look for now. When (not if) she returned, she'd know they were gone. She might accuse Wesley of hiding them first, but when they established none of them had taken it, the missing pills would draw attention to his presence.

Bobby clamped his hands on his skull, tugging at his scalp. It was already well past when he should've taken his pills, and now he couldn't even if he wanted to without putting them on alert.

"What does the door by you lead to?" Regina asked from the bottom floor. Bobby could tell which one she referred to by the way it creaked open.

"The cellar," Kerry replied.

To say Bobby had gotten lax maintaining the cellar would've been a massive understatement. He'd abandoned Pop's strict basement organization soon after his passing. His neglect had reached a level that he only remembered its existence when treating it as a dumping ground for things he hoarded, believing he'd put them to use someday.

That's it!

My old travel bag is down there, when I still used to go camping. And I always made sure to pack my prescription on those trips.

It's been so long since those trips, though. Even if a bottle had been left in there, its expiration has *to have passed by now.*

Probably. But at least it'd be something.

Bobby once again stalked around the house, doing his best to keep out of sight. He stared intently where their voices were coming from, and paid close attention to what they were saying.

If they spotted him, he had to be able to bolt immediately.

"So I was the one they chose to make an example of," Regina continued whatever story she'd been telling. "Fucking disgraceful. Revoked my track and field scholarship. Lost my full ride, and I've been struggling to make the minimum payments on my student loans since."

Bobby exhaled when he rounded the corner. He was outside the kitchen, staring at the door that led below ground to the cellar. Misty and Wesley were upstairs, and the rest of the vermin were still in the living room on the other side of the house.

They'll never even know I was inside.

"But," Kerry started, tentatively. "You *were* taking something for your training."

"Fucking disgraceful," Regina repeated, as though she hadn't heard Kerry. Angry footsteps pounded toward Bobby, paralyzing him.

"Nothing I took was on the banned substance list at the time."

Bobby heard the furious rattling of condiments as his refrigerator door was thrown open. He pressed himself tightly against the wall of the cabin. They're in the kitchen.

Regina muttered that it looked pretty bare.

"It seems rude to eat his food," Kerry mumbled.

They come to rob me, Bobby thought, but draw the line at emptying my fridge?

The kitchen floor creaked as Regina was joined by another. The footsteps sounded too heavy to belong to Kerry.

"You all right?" Decker inquired.

"Yeah." Regina sighed. "Really glad you talked me into coming. It's a relief not having to worry about paying the university back."

Bobby surmised her massive debt was the reason Regina had tagged along for this burglary. He almost felt bad she was going to walk away empty-handed.

"Seriously, why'd Brady pick *this* place?" she continued, shifting to a fuming tone. "Look around. The only thing of interest is those damn guns, and you're the only one that's into them."

Bobby glanced down at the cellar door. It was within arm's reach, and he hadn't replaced the lock since he'd lost it two years ago.

"What about the lake?" Decker commented, still calm, even in the face of her tantrum.

Bobby was always suspicious of people who were overly calm or kind. No one could stay that tranquil all the time. They *had* to get mad like everyone else. He'd seen when people like that finally lost their cool.

Their eruptions were unforgettable.

Bobby couldn't remember the door creaking, but it had been awhile since he'd gone in the cellar this way. He grasped the handle and raised it slightly.

Not even a whisper.

"What *about* it?" Regina pressed. "Just because a house is on a lake doesn't mean it's worth a damn. God, I would've thought with Wesley involved in the selection, we'd at least get something decent."

Bobby lifted the door all the way, flinching at a groan that never came. The quicker he found some pills to take, the better. He didn't want to be around when Regina found out this house held little of value.

She was liable to be more violent than Brady.

"Come on, now," Decker said, as serene as ever, even in the face of someone practically screaming at him. "Brady wouldn't've gone along with this spot if it wasn't perfect. You know the big plans he's got for this weekend."

Bobby placed a tentative foot on the top step leading to the basement. When it didn't moan beneath his weight he descended lower.

Regina scoffed above him. "Has Brady even picked a ring?" Her question drew Bobby's eyes to where

Regina and Decker were standing on the other side of the cabin wall.

There's no way Brady found Momma's jewelry box.

But you don't know how long they'd already been here before you saw them. You were too busy napping on the lake.

He replayed the first encounter he'd had with the intruders. Brady *had* come charging down the stairs to scream at Decker. With enough time to snoop around, it was possible he could've found her hoard.

"He said he had his eye on some but wanted to run them by Wesley to see which ones were the best value," Decker answered. "I don't know if Brady already spoke to him about it."

Bobby's arms started to shake under the weight of keeping the cellar door open above him. They eased the door shut each time he furthered his descent. His ribs, still sore from Brady's thrashing, joined in the chorus of agony.

He grit his teeth to combat his suffering. Half of him was still sticking out of the entryway, even when he crouched down. Once he got inside, he still had to ease the door shut. If he let it go, it would slam down above him.

Regina laughed above. "Wesley *does* love to remind everyone he comes from money."

Bobby's steps became increasingly wobbly as the trembling in his arms started to spread across the rest of his body. He nearly missed the next step and slipped down the rest of the stairs. His forehead had broken into a sweat from the exertion. He wanted to hurry, but he couldn't risk the old steps betraying him with a loud creak.

How much *longer?*

Bobby squinted past the salty perspiration stinging his eyes to count the steps he had left, and let out a soft groan. He was only halfway down the stairs, but he saw that another problem already awaited him.

The remaining sunlight had seeped into the basement from the door he was keeping ajar. He tried to recall if Regina had closed the door to the basement after confirming where it led. He couldn't remember it shutting.

One more step, and I'll be able to sit down on the stairs. I can then close the door above me, silently.

And then how will you see?

Bobby glanced down again to assess the situation. Light had poured in from the door, but the rest of the basement was shrouded in darkness. If the intruders *hadn't* closed the interior door to the basement, he wouldn't be able to turn on a light to see what he was doing.

He made up his mind to cross that bridge when he got there. Bobby extended his leg, placing a tentative step on the next plank.

Something squealed under his foot. If he'd had a hand free to steady himself along the stair rails, he could've kept his balance. But when whatever he stepped on wrestled its way out from under his weight, his foot slipped completely off the step.

His hands instinctively went to the rail, catching it before he tumbled down the stairs. Above him, the door banged shut.

11

"What was that?" Kerry shrieked upstairs.

Bobby pulled himself back to his feet as footsteps swarmed from the kitchen and living room to the basement door inside the house. The pitter-patter of the critter he'd stepped on fled across the basement. His first instinct was to go back the way he came.

He caught himself before he opened the door. Opening the door would flood the cellar with light. Bobby could run, but he used to get winded running a mile for school. Regina had been quick enough to earn a full scholarship. He doubted he'd get far.

"Did you guys hear something?" Wesley called as his footsteps galloped down from the top floor.

Bobby's eyes slowly started adjusting to the darkness. He'd accumulated plenty of junk down here since becoming a homeowner.

"It came from the basement," Regina explained.

There was a familiar click at the top of the stairs. Bobby's breath caught, until nothing happened.

"The lights must not work down there."

The temptation to run hit him like a second wave. His feet danced toward the stairs, but he forced himself to keep them planted to the ground.

Running for his life wasn't an option. Bobby knew it was crazy, but his best chance of survival was staying in the cellar.

The intruders rushed to the sound, but they haven't come—

"Someone should go down there to see what made that noise," Kerry suggested. Her voice was as shaky as ever, but she willed herself to say the words.

Really? The girl who sounds afraid of her own voice is the only one brave enough to state what needs to be done?

The urge to run overwhelmed his thoughts. He pushed the cowardice back down. Kerry might be steering them to inspect the cellar, but they hadn't come down yet.

"Are you kidding?" Wesley nearly shrieked. "Going alone to investigate a suspicious noise in the basement is a good way to get yourself killed."

Bobby grew more comfortable hiding in the dark. His night vision made out most of his surroundings. He was familiar with the basement. They weren't. In the dark, that gave him an advantage.

But you keep a flashlight in the kitchen. They've surely spotted it by now, his inner demon reminded him.

"You're free to join me," Kerry said dryly.

Bobby fought the itch to escape again. Even with nothing between him and the door, he couldn't run. He had to assume if they came down to search the cellar, they'd have his flashlight. His only option was to hide.

He scrambled to think where to go. There was plenty of junk to hide behind, but if they came down with a light, they were sure to check behind everything. He'd have to keep moving without making a sound if he wanted to evade them.

"I should really stay up here in case Misty needs me," Wesley said hurriedly. The pace with which he flew back up the stairs was even faster.

Bobby pressed himself to remember what was down here. Pop's old workbench was close by, but it couldn't provide him with any cover. There was an old fridge that had died two years ago that Bobby hadn't gotten around to removing. That was no good, either.

If he tried to move it from the wall to create a hiding spot for himself, they were bound to hear.

"What about *you* two?" Kerry asked upstairs.

The old crawl space.

Bobby's eyes snapped through the darkness to his favorite hiding spot growing up. When he was a kid, his cousins would come to visit for two weeks each summer, and they used to love playing hide-and-seek. Bobby's favorite place to hide was a small cutout along the wall in a corner of the cellar. He chuckled over the memory of them never being able to find him. It had felt spacious as a child. He hoped that it was still roomy enough to fit him now.

"I really don't think it was anything," Regina said. "I think we just got startled is all. Old places like this creak and make weird noises all the time."

Bobby's smile faltered. The crawl space was on the opposite side of the cellar, which he'd cluttered over the years. He now had to wade through a labyrinth of garbage to get to it.

In the dark.

"It was *more* than just a creak," Kerry protested. Her voice was still soft, but for the first time, Bobby heard a slight edge to it.

These hardened criminals turn into cowards the second they hear a bump in the night.

Go! Go now. While they're still squabbling with each other.

Bobby trekked toward the crawl space as soundlessly as he could. He lifted his feet slightly off the ground to keep them from dragging across the floor. Each tentative step was placed gently to keep from tripping over the rubbish he'd polluted the basement with. His arms waved in front of him, probing for any piles he might bump into.

It was slow going.

"If something was down there, we would've heard it make another sound by now," Decker tried to reassure Kerry.

Almost on cue, Bobby's hand brushed against the top of one of the piles. He felt the peak start to tip over. Both hands shot through the dark to grab it before it toppled to the ground. It felt like a model airplane he'd built nearly two decades ago. He settled it on the ground and moved on.

"I don't think I'll be able to sleep without knowing for sure," Kerry insisted.

The mountains of discarded knickknacks closed in on him the closer he got to the crawlspace. Pop's constant lectures to take care of the house echoed through his head, mocking him.

This is what you get for being a crybaby over maintaining the cellar. A trybaby would've kept this place in order and wouldn't have this problem.

His hand settled on the wall above the crawl space. He breathed a sigh of relief as he pawed his way down to the hole in the wall. Bobby felt a slight draft and knew he was close. He continued swatting at the wall until he came up empty.

Jackpot.

Bobby crouched down to sit in front of the opening. It was partially blocked by one of the mounds of junk. This tower of trash was light, and he had no problem lifting it and clearing the entrance to the crawlspace. He felt around to see if it was as wide as he remembered.

Was it always this small?

He desperately slid feet first into the crawlspace. By the time his hips reached the opening, his toes touched a cardboard box he didn't remember being there as a kid. Bobby reminded himself he was a lot taller now, and that his legs wouldn't have gone that far within the crawlspace when he was a child. He tried to lift his leg over the box, and found the wall.

"If you really need to go down there to investigate . . . ." Decker started to say.

Bobby turned to the stairs in horror. Decker's tone suggested Kerry had swayed him into searching the basement with her. The way he'd spoken about hunting, Bobby didn't think he stood a chance if Decker came down.

"Take this with you," Decker finished his thought. A moment later, a beam of light shone down into the basement.

They'd found the flashlight.

"Thanks," Kerry muttered, in a tone that was anything but gracious.

Steps receded back into the living room, leaving Kerry by herself at the top of the stairs. She sighed deeply and descended into the cellar.

She kept the light in front of her, but Bobby suspected she'd check every corner before she was satisfied nothing was down here. Even behind a couple heaps of junk, he felt exposed.

"This is what you get," Kerry muttered aloud to herself as she reached the second step from the top.

Bobby started to crawl back out of the wall, stopping when he felt a tug. He turned back over his shoulder, but couldn't make out what the problem was in the blackness.

He pressed forward again and got nowhere. The entrance to the crawlspace squeezed him as he tried to slip free.

Stuck!

"Knew this wasn't the crowd I wanted to get in with," Kerry continued, taking another two steps.

Bobby squirmed, tugged, and yanked as silently as he could, still not wanting to draw her attention. There were only five more steps until Kerry was in the basement. He prayed she'd abandon her cause before she reached that point.

"All they care about is filling their wallets or when they're getting their next fix."

Four steps.

He dug his nails dug into the ground attempting to free himself from the mouth of the opening. Bobby clamped his mouth shut to stifle a whimper as the wall that held him slowly peeled skin off his thigh. A tear forged a path past his closed eyelids and down his cheek.

"Regina pumping anything into her body that builds mass. Misty taking anything she can get her hands on. That is, when she's not going for a cleanse at some fancy rehab center." She snorted. "*Which* she treats like a spa. And a nightclub."

Three steps.

There was a faint pitter-patter by the stairs. The rodent he'd slipped on falling into the cellar had taken up shelter under the stairs leading upstairs. As Kerry came down the stairs, it darted away from her, toward Bobby.

Its scampering sounded deafening. Kerry was bound to hear it and swing the light in his direction.

It's over. It's all over. They got you now.

"Or they're a sadistic psychopath like Decker. How many stories *could* he have shared about trapping and killing animals?"

Two steps.

His ears tracked the scurrying across the floor. He raised his arm above his hills of hoarding, unconcerned about Kerry flashing the light his way, and swatted down at the critter, grabbing a firm hold of it around its neck. The last thing he needed was for it to start squealing.

"Or they're Wesley with his grand plans for spending Daddy's money. And Brady." She had to pause before she went on. "The way he's obsessed with other people's money now. . . . He practically follows Wesley everywhere, obeying his every command like a puppy. That need for money . . . it's *changed him.*"

One step.

The critter was bigger than he'd expected. It wrestled to free itself from his firm grasp. He grabbed its hind legs with his other hand to keep it from clawing at the palm of his hand as it struggled for leverage to yank its head free.

"How long have you been telling yourself you wanted to end things with Brady? Why'd you let him convince you there was anything he could do to inject any glimmer of hope beyond this weekend? Why do you *keep* letting him talk you into doing things you don't . . . *want* . . . to . . . *do*!"

Her feet touched down on the basement floor.

"Stop making excuses. Start standing *up* for yourself."

Teeth clamped down on his finger. One hand shot to his mouth to silence his screech.

The beam of light swung in his direction.

12

One of the stacks of boxes filled with long-forgotten items blocked him from Kerry's view. The protection they provided wouldn't last. Her footsteps rushed to the corner he was hiding in.

The vermin continued to claw and gnaw at his hand. He couldn't take it anymore.

Bobby flung the rodent in the direction of the light, skipping it across the ground. The light darted to the sound of its shriek. A moment later, the pitter-patter resumed, dashing to the other side of the cellar.

Please think my screech was the critter. Please think my screech was the critter. *Please* think my screech was the critter.

Kerry howled. The light wobbled all around the room as it bounced off the ground. Above, footsteps raced to the cellar door, intercepting Kerry as she bounded up the stairs.

"Kerry, what was it?" Regina asked, trying to calm her down.

Bobby didn't dwell on his success. He ripped himself out from the wall, grimacing as it tore at his thigh. The flashlight settled, lighting up a path in front of him. He hobbled his way through the labyrinth of trash as fast as he could. His shoulder brushed up against one of the heaps. Bobby blindly grabbed at one of the falling items, nabbing a screwdriver. What sounded like a small cardboard box hit the ground.

Decker cleared his throat. "I heard some—"

"Rats!" Kerry wailed above. "This place has *rats!*"

Bobby took the stairs leading out the back quickly, but quietly.

Doesn't matter that you don't make a noise if they see the dwindling sunlight fill the cellar when you open the door, his inner demon antagonized him.

I'm dead anyway, if I stay down here.

"What's all the screaming about?" Wesley asked in a quavering voice from the top floor.

Bobby popped through the cellar door leading back outside. Twilight had set in rapidly since he'd entered the basement. He doubted any light had shined through the open door.

"There're *rats!*" Kerry screamed. "What kind of place did you bring us to?"

He took care to ease the door closed. Everyone had converged around Kerry. No one was chasing after him. As far as he knew, they weren't even aware of his presence.

He intended to keep it that way.

"Now wait just a minute," Wesley said, defensively. Footsteps galloped down the stairs to join the rest of the party.

Are they all downstairs now? Bobby wondered.

His eyes shot up to the top floor. The windows were still wide open. Even in the dusk, Bobby stayed low to the ground until he was behind the tree between the two guestrooms.

"I only went along with Brady because he was *adamant* about this place," Wesley yelled.

Bobby did his best to ignore the shouting match, which was impossible. Their voices carried perfectly through all the open windows. He strained his ears to pick up any sound from the top floor.

"You gotta admit, this place has *nothing*," Regina snapped.

You might not get a better chance to get to your pills.

Ascending the tree wasn't as smooth this time. He'd scraped the skin off his thigh getting out of the crawlspace. He felt a slight burn every time he raised his leg to climb higher.

"*Brady* picked this place!" Wesley insisted. His tone was a worthy challenger to any playground debate. "He kept saying it reminded him of the places he and Decker used to go to when they were younger."

Bobby's ribs gave him the most trouble. It was the first time he'd put them to use since Brady's beating. He noticed for the first time that he'd been hunched over since the attack because he couldn't stand up straight. When he pulled himself higher up the trunk, his upper body retracted into the fetal position. His reach became more and more limited the higher he scaled the tree.

He took a moment to catch his breath when he reached the branch outside the guestroom next to Pop's. His clothes clung to him, held tightly by his sweat.

"But you're always talking about enjoying the finer things," Regina shot back. "What'd you think a dump like this had to offer?"

If there's nothing here you want, then leave me alone!

They'll never leave you be. You killed one of them.

His legs wobbled as he balanced on the branch, and his perspiration stung his scraped thigh. He doubted his ability to make it in through the window.

"I want to get out of here," Kerry stated boldly. It was the first time, outside of her shouts about the rats, that Bobby didn't detect a trace of meekness.

His reservations mounted the longer he stood on the branch. His frayed thigh shook so bad the branch started to bounce.

"We're *not* going anywhere," Wesley snarled.

Bobby flailed his arms to keep his equilibrium. His body threatened to tumble off the branch.

Climb in already! They'll hear the thud if I drop.

Won't matter when the fall breaks your neck.

Shut *up*!

He leaned forward, catching the window frame of the guestroom next to Pop's room softly with his hands. The wood barely grunted. Bobby thrust his wounded leg onto the window sill, making sure his footing was secure before he abandoned the branch completely.

"I don't care what Brady had planned for this weekend," Kerry said below him.

Bobby would have sworn he was listening to a new woman.

Bobby tested the floorboards with a probing step. They didn't even emit a whisper under his weight. He grinned in the darkness, believing he could grab his medication from the bathroom and go without them ever knowing.

Then he'd knock on neighbor's doors until one was home, and convince them to call the authorities. Not Knotts. The *state* police.

"Oh, yeah? And where did you intend to go?" Wesley challenged her. "Do you have any money to rent a hotel? To pay for a ride there? To get back home?"

Bobby snickered at their bickering. This was almost going to be too easy.

Misty breezed past the bedroom door.

Bobby tensed up like a rabbit ready to bolt after spotting a predator. She didn't seem to notice him as she glided toward the stairs. He promised himself he'd been shrouded in the darkness of the room as she'd passed by. His assurances did nothing to slow down his racing heart.

"Everything okay down there?" Misty called down the stairs.

He poked his head out the bedroom door. Misty was leaning over the top of the stairs. Instead of joining them downstairs, or even descending a step or two, she craned her neck at an awkward angle to get a look under the balcony at them.

"We're fine," Decker said, in that calming tone of his. "Kerry just saw—"

"Rats!" Kerry started up again. "I don't know what your boyfriend was thinking, choosing this place."

Bobby willed Misty to head downstairs to join her friends. Misty didn't move. She just strained her neck even farther when Kerry spoke, presumably to see who was talking.

Misty giggled. "He's not my—"

"*I* didn't want this place!" Wesley shouted, cutting her off.

Bobby crept out into the hall. Misty wasn't budging from the top of the stairs. His odds were better going for the pills now while she was distracted with all the shouting, than continuing to wait for her to join her comrades downstairs. In all likelihood, one of the intruders would accompany her upstairs before she returned to them below.

"Besides, it's fine up here," Wesley continued. "It's only the basement that has rats, and there's nothing worth going in the basement for."

Bobby snuck down the hallway with ease. His years of growing up in this house had taught him all the cabin's secrets, including which floorboards moaned when he put weight on them. Even in darkness, his selection of where to tiptoe was flawless.

The light in the bathroom was left on, and Bobby assumed this was where Misty had come from. Her back was still to him as he stepped into the only part of the hallway that was lit. He ducked into the room quickly before she had a chance to turn around and spot him.

Now you just need the same luck getting out of here as you did getting in.

First things first.

Bobby couldn't remember if the medicine cabinet whined when it opened. Taking no chances, he cradled it with both hands and slowly pried it open.

His face dropped. The cabinet was lined with prescriptions, both new and expired, but there was one gap among the ranks. He immediately knew it was the one bottle he'd come for.

Before he could growl that one of them had taken it, the determined thuds of footsteps advanced toward the bathroom.

13

They trapped me!

You trapped yourself.

His escape was cut off. The moment he stepped into the hallway, the bathroom light would become a spotlight centered on him. He couldn't turn the light off now without arousing suspicion. Even if Misty was too scared to investigate a light suddenly going out by herself, if she called for help, he still had no way of getting out. There was no tree outside the bathroom window to climb down.

There was the possibility that she was heading to Pop's room, which did nothing to comfort him. She might have walked by him when he was in the guestroom, but he'd been standing in the dark. He'd be pressing his luck trying to exit the bathroom without her hearing the door open or seeing him coming out.

His eyes scrambled for a hiding spot. The only option they could see was to hide in his bathtub. The curtains around it had been half drawn. As long as she didn't stay in there with him too long, he felt he stood a chance.

She still hasn't taken that shower.

Lucky you. You finally get to bathe with a woman.

He turned for the tub and stopped short. The medicine cabinet was still open. Bobby eased it shut and jumped behind the curtain as the steps in the hallway reached the door.

The bathroom floorboards moaned under Misty's soft footsteps. Bobby pressed himself up against the tiled wall, holding both hands over his mouth to keep himself from making a peep.

"Misty, everything all right up there?" Decker called up the stairs.

Bobby's heart hammered at the inside of his chest. The last thing he wanted was for Decker to be close by if Misty found him. His mind played out every possible escape route he could take if he had to run.

None of them ended well.

"I'm *fine*," she insisted a little too forcefully. "All the yelling's exacerbated my headache. I'm looking for something to take for it."

Bobby waited with Misty for a response. All they could hear was the continued arguing below. They both panicked at the sound of Decker advancing up the stairs.

"I'll join you guys if you can just give all the shouting a rest!" Misty snapped.

Decker's pace paused at the top of the stairs. Misty was on the verge of hyperventilating. Bobby felt she was more terrified than he was.

Finally, the wooden stairs shifted under Decker's weight as he called out, "Guys, why don't we start negotiating a truce?" before descending back down the stairs.

Misty let out a deep sigh. Bobby allowed himself to breathe. He forced himself to keep the exhalation below a whisper. Bobby wasn't sure how she didn't hear the jackhammering of his heart, but he wasn't about to test how loud he could get without her noticing.

Regina scoffed from the kitchen when Decker told them Misty was searching for something for her headache. "If anyone knows their way around medication, its Misty," she sniped.

"Bitch," Misty muttered.

They're constantly at each other's throats.

Bobby gulped and rubbed at his own neck to make sure it was still safe. It snapped toward a familiar rattle.

She's got my pills!

"Don't act like you're a stranger to pharmaceuticals," Wesley shouted at Regina.

Misty popped the cap off and poured a couple tablets onto the sink. Bobby found it curious why she didn't dispense them into her hand.

"What'd you say, little man?" Regina barked. Bobby swore he heard Wesley yelp, and imagined he'd found something to cower behind.

He wished they'd stop yelling downstairs so he could focus on what Misty was up to. Putting the capsules on the sink was odd enough, but she also wasn't running any water to wash them down.

On the other side of the curtain, porcelain scraped against itself. Misty grunted, and Bobby pieced together that she'd removed the lid of the toilet's tank. A moment later, he heard the crunch of the pills being ground to dust as Misty crushed them up with the lid.

"Let's all take it easy," Decker said, playing the peacemaker.

Misty restored the lid to its proper place. She pawed at it long enough for Bobby to figure out she was clearing off any debris from the capsules, making sure she left no trace. She sucked on her fingers once she was done, not wanting to leave a single crumb.

With the pills converted into powder, Misty began snorting her concoction. She made short work of it, inhaling it faster than a vacuum.

"I'm calm," Kerry insisted. "So long as nobody tries to stop me."

Bobby was appalled at how quickly Misty had gotten high. His imagination ran wild as he tried to envision how many tablets had spilled out onto the sink. He took one pill every twelve hours. She had definitely poured out more than that.

Two? Three?

Count yourself lucky if it was no more than five.

"*You're* going to be the one to tell Brady then!" Wesley screamed. "Don't leave it to the rest of us to deal with his temper when he finds out."

Bobby had just refilled the prescription this past week. Even as poor as his math was, he knew he'd still have plenty left over after Misty's fix.

If this was the only time she got high. The comments the other intruders had made suggested Misty had built up a tolerance.

"I can't call him. The battery died on my phone straining to get a reception," Kerry replied. The rest of them muttered their phones had met similar fates. "He'd promised he wasn't going to leave me alone with a bunch of people I didn't know. Why should I be concerned about his feelings when he *never* cares about mine?"

Mr. Manning will understand if I come to him looking for a refill so soon. He'll understand when I tell him about the intruders.

Ha! Every time you walk in there for a refill, Mr. Manning sees the same five-year-old who stole from a basket of penny candies and got snared in his own lie.

Amid the sniffling Misty was doing, the medicine cabinet didn't open. Bobby feared Misty wasn't done with his meds.

"Brady's not back yet?" Decker noted. His observation was quickly swallowed by the continued quarreling.

"How do you expect to leave, then?" Wesley demanded.

"The phone's right there," Kerry pointed out. "There's bound to be a phone book somewhere. I'll book a place for myself, and call a cab. Hopefully my credit card doesn't get declined. What's another couple hundred dollars added to my mountain of loans?"

The bottle of pills rattled again, this time sounding muffled. Bobby envisioned Misty stuffing his prescription into her pocket. He heard a few more sniffs while she patted her hair.

She's trying to make herself look presentable so the rest don't get wise to her dirty little secret.

"Kerry," Regina jumped in, "I don't like this place either, but . . . maybe Wesley's right." The way she finished the thought, Bobby could tell she would've preferred swallowing acid over agreeing with the prick.

Misty went still for a moment, and Bobby tensed up, fearing she'd noticed she wasn't alone. She then began to giggle giddily.

"But be reasonable about this," Regina continued. "Brady told us about how much you've been juggling graduating and working as much as you could to take care of your mom's bills. He was adamant that this weekend was for you."

The bathroom door opened. Misty did her best to stifle her chuckling, but that only put her in another titter. Her footsteps receded into the hallway.

I've got to get my pills from her.

Bobby emerged from the tub, but stopped himself from leaving the bathroom when he saw Misty just standing in the middle of the hall, giggling uncontrollably. He was worried she might spot his shadow as he closed in on her until he saw it was a struggle for her to keep her balance.

"Maybe it'd be best not to set yourself back even further," Regina suggested.

Misty bumped into the doorframe as she wandered aimlessly into Pop's room. She didn't even seem fazed; she just continued into the bedroom and swung her arm at the wall until she flipped on the light switch.

Bobby closed the bathroom door behind him silently. He wasn't worried about the intruders below hearing it. They'd assume it was Misty. Misty was most likely too strung out to even notice him before he got to her, but now that he was this close, he didn't want to risk tipping her off.

As he followed her into Pop's room, Misty nearly stumbled into the antlers of Pop's prized buck. Pop had always preached against the vice of pride, yet the low placement of the deer head suggested that even the old man had succumbed to vanity. Bobby had caught Pop, more than once, admiring himself in the dresser mirror, pretending to stroke the antlers that were hanging on the wall behind him, like they were a crown. She came up short, smirked at the display, and playfully poked one of the tips.

Bobby was sure she wasn't aware of his presence. The thought was confirmed when she fumbled to pull her shirt over her head. His first thought was how milky smooth her skin looked. His second was that she wasn't wearing a bra.

Maybe she'll turn around and you'll get a great view before she shrieks at the sight of you. How quick do you think the rest of them can bolt up—

Bobby covered up her mouth with his palm while his other hand fished through her pocket for his drugs. He felt her grow alert in his grasp.

He took his eyes off her to measure the distance to Pop's door. There was no doubt she'd call for help as soon as he let her go, and he wanted to gage how far he could get before they came after him. He thought he could make it out the window before they got up the stairs, though he didn't like his chances of scrambling down the tree before they got outside.

They won't stop chasing you. You've seen too much.

Bobby had been contemplating dragging her with him until he reached the guest bedroom. He'd have to let her go once he climbed out the window, and she would shout to the others where to head him off. He wouldn't get much more of a head start, but even a few fractions of a second were worth it.

None of it mattered. Whether she had picked up that he wasn't giving her his full attention, or she panicked that a stranger had grabbed her from behind and was now sliding his hand to her pocket, her instinct to fight kicked in.

She wrenched her right arm free from her sleeve and flung it wildly behind her. Bobby grunted as she connected with his ribs, still tender from his encounter with Brady.

"I don't think I should've come here in the first place," Kerry's voice carried from downstairs. They were all still oblivious to what was going on above.

Bobby's grip slipped from her mouth. Seizing her freedom, Misty charged from her captor. One of the points of the antlers stabbed through her shirt just above her shoulder. Bobby cringed. Had she charged into it slightly to the right she would have collided with the antlers neck first.

"Did Brady tell any of you that it took a month before he finally wore me down to do this?" Kerry asked the rest of the gang.

Misty staggered back from the display, favoring her shoulder. Bobby could see the tip of the point that had pierced her shirt had dampened. His eyes were immediately drawn away as she turned around.

Hypnotic rubies!

She still wrestled beneath the shirt to get it off her head, and Bobby could see her loading up a scream. His hand shot to cover her mouth.

"Brady framed this whole trip like it would be doing you a lot of good," Decker answered Kerry.

Misty bit down through her shirt, nipping Bobby's fingers. He pulled his hand away, knowing she'd keep snapping until her teeth clamped down on his digits. She started to load up another scream, which he cut off when he grabbed her by the throat.

Her left arm was still raised above her head, trapped in the sleeve she was trying to wrestle out of.

She used her free hand to swing at his head, connecting twice before he could fend her off.

The shirt she was ensnared in slipped down the right side of her face, low enough to expose her eye. Bobby saw she was terrified.

And determined.

Kerry laughed below. "Of course! He's *never* the bad guy."

Still striking him with her right hand, she opened wide to screech. Bobby realized his grip had loosened and squeezed her neck to cut off the scream in her throat, surprising himself with how tightly he could choke her.

Her frenzied attacks intensified. She hammered down on his arm repeatedly. He had a huge size advantage over her, yet felt she was doing all the damage, even as her eyes were going blank.

"Please stop fighting," he cried softly, his voice so low he merely mouthed the words. "I don't want to kill you. I don't. I just want my pills."

She continued to struggle in his grasp. Her face purpled. Bobby wanted to let her go, but feared the voracity of the attacks she'd unleash if he released her.

Knotts didn't just send thieves. He sent killers.

Her swipes started to slow. He could feel her gulping for air in his palm. She chopped down on his arm. It was her hardest yet. Again, harder still. Again. This time the impact felt weaker.

She'll pass out first before you choke the life out her.

Misty hacked feebly at him. His arm didn't even budge on impact. Bobby glanced at Pop's bed. He'd retrieve his pills and tuck her in for the night. She'd wake up with a sore throat, but she'd be fine.

Until he had her arrested, anyway.

With a last ditch effort, Misty reared back and kicked at Bobby. Her foot struck him squarely in the kneecap, knocking his own leg out from under him.

Bobby lost his balance and fell forward, driving Misty back toward the wall. He wasn't aware he still had her by the throat until the tip of the antler stabbed his palm, jarring his grip loose.

Misty's right eye went wide as he shoved her neck through the antler. When Bobby's hand slipped from her windpipe, she let out the beginning of a death scream that was cut off immediately as she gurgled on her own blood.

Bobby could only gape as the shirt she was tangled in began to darken. The mount couldn't support her dead weight, and her lifeless body crashed to the ground. He didn't need to worry about whether the intruders below heard the thump.

Their bickering had stopped at the sound of her scream.

14

A stampede trampled up the stairs, converging on Pop's room. Bobby had no time to tremble like a cornered rat. He had to get out of there.

The only light in the hallway came from Pop's room, and from the other side of the closed bathroom door. The rest of the top floor was shrouded in darkness. Bobby scurried into the nearest guestroom and hid in the corner. His only chance of survival depended on them being drawn to the lights.

Images of Misty flashed through his mind. Tears rained from his eyes, but he covered his mouth to keep from sobbing.

Don't mourn her. She was here to rob you. To kill *you.*

That doesn't make what I did right!

The parade of intruders charged down the hall to Pop's room. He pressed himself tight to the corner as his eyes darted to the open window.

"How long've you been carrying that—"

Kerry stopped asking her question as the first footsteps rushed into Pop's room. Bobby stared at the wall where he expected them to be standing.

"Oh, god," Regina muttered on the other side of the wall.

Regina was gagging before being joined by one of her cohorts. A third set of steps entered the room. Bobby recognized Kerry's screams.

You killed that poor girl for nothing. You didn't even get your meds from her.

Bobby winced at the realization. There was no going back for them now. The only choice he had left was to run and convince someone to call the state police.

And pray people believed him when he said the two deaths had been accidents.

He cradled his battered arm close to his chest, and favored his kicked knee, hobbling silently to the window. One look at the distance to the branch was enough to convince him he couldn't reach it. Not with his knee already swelling up, limiting the range he could bend it, and the amount of weight he trusted putting on it.

The tree outside his bedroom was the only way out. It would still be a struggle to shimmy down, but the trunk was right outside his window. If this window was open, that one had to be, too.

"What happened?" Wesley called tentatively from the stairs.

Bobby froze in the window. The coward hadn't run toward the danger like the others.

"It's . . . Misty," Regina choked out. "It's . . . awful!"

Wesley hurried up the stairs. He passed the room Bobby was hiding in without a glance. "Did she OD?" he asked before turning into Pop's room. "I *knew* she was using a—"

Bobby lurked toward the door of the guestroom. As far as he could tell, they were all in Pop's room. If he was right about that, he had a clear path to his bedroom and down the tree.

"Brady's going to kill someone," Wesley stated.

That's where their minds go to first? Bobby wondered. Murder?

With each stride, Bobby wished he'd put carpeting down in the bedrooms. Every step risked a groan from the floorboards, and they only needed to hear one of them. The bedroom door felt a mile away as he slowed his pace even further in an effort not to upset the aging wood.

The intruders showed no concern about making noise. The floorboards in Pop's room creaked, presumably under the weight of one of them getting a closer inspection of Misty's lifeless body.

Less than a foot of timber separates you from those maniacs.

"I don't think you have to worry about Brady," Decker said flatly.

Decker's tone hadn't changed from when Bobby had first heard him speak, and that terrified Bobby even more. Before, there'd been no reason for Decker to lose his composure. The others complained, even shouted, about their problems, but none of their issues affected what he'd come here to do. But now, he was examining a dead body, someone he'd known well enough to travel out of state with, and he still spoke in that level tone.

What was worse was that, with that statement, Bobby realized that Decker discerned Brady was dead. Decker knew two of them were dead, and he spoke about it the same way he'd ask someone to pass the ketchup at a diner.

If Bobby's knee had allowed it, he would've bolted for the door just to get as far from Decker as fast as he could.

"What do you—?" Kerry started, before her voice trailed off. "Oh . . . oh, god."

Now she knows, too.

The door was within arm's reach, and Bobby began estimating how many more steps he had to take to get to his bedroom window. As though sensing his flight wasn't hard enough, his limp worsened with each step.

"He'll be back soon from getting sup—"

Regina swallowed her words. Bobby took it to mean she understood Brady was gone, too.

He probed for the doorframe to ensure he didn't collide into it. Any thump the intruders heard would put an immediate end to his escape.

"What is it?" Wesley asked. He spoke with an awareness that he wasn't privy to knowledge everyone else had.

Bobby popped his head out of the room, trusting that it would be too dark in the hallway for them to catch the movement. The hall was vacant, except for the shadows they cast from Pop's room. He had a clear path to his room.

"The van's still here," Kerry reminded Wesley.

Wesley gasped when the conclusion hit him.

Bobby rooted himself to the floor as the moaning of dead lumber drew nearer to Pop's door. He had just stepped out into the hallway, and could see the shadows from his father's room getting bigger. He was certain it was Wesley approaching the door, looking to escape. Scenarios raced through Bobby's head, too fast for his mind to process. If the arrogant coward ran out of the room, things would get complicated. He'd have to retreat back into the guestroom, but he'd have to sacrifice stealth for speed. The rest of them might mistake the sound of his footsteps for Wesley's, but Wesley wouldn't. The chickenshit would probably reveal Bobby's location to his cronies while still fleeing from danger.

"How hard would you have to push to do that to her?" Regina observed.

Bobby winced, wishing they would stop making comments that would terrify Wesley further. The punk had stopped in Pop's doorway while his shadow danced in the hall. Bobby couldn't tell if Wesley was about to bolt from the room or not, which led to his own indecision over whether to retreat or press on toward his room. Wesley would crash into him if he dashed for the exit. But if Bobby stayed in the guestroom too long, he'd risk being found.

The unlit hall had halted Wesley's flight. If Wesley had been able to see, Bobby had no doubt he'd still be running. With the uncertainty of the darkness, Wesley had chosen the safety provided by the group.

That settled things for Bobby. He took another cautious step toward his bedroom.

"Wait," Kerry said. "If somebody did this . . . where is he?"

They know I'm here.

They'd tear this place apart looking for you if you didn't make it so easy for them standing there waiting.

Bobby was now in the middle of the hall. They were still in Pop's room, and he was still in the darkness, but that could all change in an instant. There was a light switch right outside Pop's room. His knee barked at him, reminding him it'd be slow going if he had to run.

"No one got past us as we were coming up," Wesley said in a quivering voice. Bobby suspected that it had hit home to Wesley that holding back while the rest of them had rushed to Misty's scream had turned out to be the most dangerous thing he could have done. If her killer was loose in the house, his cowardice had put him in jeopardy by separating himself from the group.

Bobby took another two steps and settled his hands against the door of Pop's study. He was one door away from his room.

"It *did* take us a bit to get up here," Decker said thoughtfully. "He could've snuck into one of the rooms up here—"

The words made Bobby's stomach ball up into a tight knot. He was so close, but the years spent living here had taught him the floorboards became a minefield of creaks and moans the closer he got to the stairs. He had to slow down even more not to aggravate the timber beneath his feet.

If they flip the lights on now . . . .

"The bathroom lights're on!" Wesley let out a high-strung shout. "If he's here, we've got him cornered!"

The triumph in Wesley's voice, now that he believed the threat was at a disadvantage, spooked Bobby, making him rush his next step. The floor whispered beneath his feet. He clutched the doorframe of his room because he couldn't think of anything else to do. The intruders gave no indication they'd heard.

That's your one freebie. Next time, they'll come and kill you.

"If he *did* get by us," Decker continued, as though Wesley hadn't interrupted him, "there's nothing between him and the guns."

Bobby stood inside the doorway to his own bedroom. He was one step away from no longer being out in the open, but making for the guns sounded like the better option. Getting his hands on them would tip the scales in his favor. It wouldn't matter that there were four of them and only one of him. They'd surrender if he aimed one of Pop's rifles at them. Wesley definitely would. Kerry would be sensible enough, too. So would Regina. Decker, he wasn't so sure about. He'd put Decker down if he had to.

Having possession of Pop's guns also kept them out of their hands. He gathered from Decker's bear-hunting story that he knew how to track an animal, and Bobby didn't doubt he could do it in the dark.

"So I'll go down and get them," Regina cut Wesley off, who was in the middle of making the same offer. His voice had receded back to tininess now that it wasn't a certainty Misty's killer was trapped.

Bobby was on the edge of the steps, trying to calculate if he could make it down to the gun case before they did. Even with his head start, it would be a close race.

"Not alone, you're not," Decker barked sharply, though his snarl sounded more protective than angry.

Bobby planted a toe on the top step when a thought came to him. Ammunition was always close by, but Pop never kept the rifles loaded when they were in the house.

They won't know that. They'll be too busy pissing themselves when the gun is pointed at their faces.

Does Decker look like someone who hasn't calmly stared down the barrel of a gun? What're you gonna do if he forces you to pull the trigger and the rest of 'em see nothing happens?

"*I'll* go with her," Wesley exclaimed, cutting off Kerry's bid to volunteer.

"Fine. Someone needs to stay with Decker, anyway," Kerry said, glaring at Wesley. "Just hurry up and do it already."

Bobby could tell both Kerry and Wesley were scared. It was clear neither had broken into someone's home before. Kerry's earlier comments confirmed she'd been dragged into this. The more Wesley spoke, the less Bobby believed he was the son of a don, revising his assumption to Wesley being the son of a lawyer. Wesley definitely came from money, and Bobby felt he was only doing this for the thrills. He may have been willing to have risked getting caught because he trusted his daddy to bail him out, but getting killed? Wesley couldn't get away fast enough.

Shuffling came from Pop's room. An arm reached through the doorway for the lights.

15

"Regina!" Decker called to her as the hall lit up.

Bobby watched as Regina ducked her head back into Pop's room before noticing him out in the open. He nearly vaulted into his bedroom before she had a chance to poke her head out again.

"Take this," Decker continued.

Gasps came from Pop's room. Bobby cringed, not wanting to know what Decker was offering her.

And less so the more they spoke.

"Look at the size of that thing!" Wesley exclaimed. "Do you carry that with you everywhere?"

"Yes," Decker stated bluntly. "Never know. It's great for skinning all *kinds* of things."

Bobby's skin went cold from the inside. His imagination ran wild picturing the size of the blade.

He nearly tripped on something as he made for the window. Reaching down, he felt the suitcase Wesley had tossed into his room.

That felt like days ago now.

Fool! He stuffed something in here when Knotts noticed it. Maybe it's a weapon you can use to defend yourself.

"What about you?" Regina asked.

Bobby's hands explored for the latches to the suitcase. His palms muffled their unfastening.

"I've got my own protection."

Bobby didn't want to stick around long enough to learn what that meant. He softly padded the contents of the suitcase. Most of it was clothing. There was one apparatus made of glass. The more he felt it, the more he believed it was a bong.

No tools to burgle my house?

Stop wasting time. Get out. NOW!

"Wait," Decker said, stopping the footsteps that had marched out into the hall. "If we're going to split up, everyone keep at least one other person in sight. I'll station myself here. If Wesley's right and he didn't get by us when we ran up here, we've got him cornered in the bathroom, and I won't move in until we've got our hands on the guns."

Bobby thought the panicked shuffling was coming from his own feet until he heard Wesley speak.

"What if," the brat started, already on edge, "that maniac already grabbed the guns while we've been wasting time dicking around?"

Nothing would've pleased Bobby more than to have had his hands on Pop's rifles. Preferably loaded. He'd have them lying face first on the floor, waiting for the cops to come haul them away. And he'd retrieve his pills from Misty. He couldn't shake the feeling all his problems would go away if he had a gun.

"We'll cross that bridge when we have to," Decker explained.

Bobby would've never guessed Decker was standing over a corpse with how calmly he spoke. He crept to the window as the footsteps started down the hall again.

Decker's voice stopped them all. "And let's be safe and check the rooms as we pass them."

You waited too long. You waited too long and now they're going to find you. Decker's gonna carve you open, and you'll only be able to watch as he pulls—

The creaks from the guestroom brought him back to reality. They were inspecting the room he had just come from. Pop's study would be next. If he was lucky, they'd investigate the guestroom across the hall before checking his room.

He needed to be gone before they did.

His knee howled as he stepped onto his windowsill. It wobbled as he extended his good leg to the awaiting branch. His inner demons kept chanting that he was going to lose his balance and plummet to his death. They promised it would be quick, and that at least he would avoid being tortured by the intruders when they found him.

"Clear," Regina called from across the hall.

Bobby bent his bad knee as far as it could, preparing to pounce onto the tree. It barely budged, giving his body pause. He looked down the trunk of the tree. Even though he'd mastered scaling down it quickly, he knew this time it'd be slow going. He believed he'd still be visible from the window by the time they reached his room.

The lights in Pop's study came on.

His knee started to shake. He grabbed the overhang of the roof to steady himself. His eyes shot to the lumber above him with a new idea.

It would take at least ten feet of climbing down the tree to reach the ground. All he had to do was hoist himself up onto the roof. He'd risk them hearing him above, but the logs Pop had used for the roof were thick, and absorbed a lot of sound made on top of it. There were times when the windows were closed that Bobby had had no idea it was pouring outside until he looked out a window.

You ain't exactly the most observant fella. Besides, all the windows are open. They'll hear you scampering across the top.

They're making so much noise. Maybe they'll be so busy looking for me they won't even hear me climbing up there.

"Clear," Regina announced.

Bobby didn't see another choice. He swung his good leg from the branch to the side of the house. Planting his leg delicately against the wall, he grabbed the overhang with both hands and heaved himself onto the roof. Most of himself. His legs dangled over the edge.

He clawed at the roof for something to pull himself up with. The wood was too smooth to offer assistance. Bobby shifted his hips so he could start swinging his legs from side to side, building enough momentum for him to vault them onto the roof. He panicked as the maneuver caused him to slide back over the ledge.

"Clear," Regina declared from across the hall.

Bobby's good leg found the wall again. With a forceful push, he sprang onto the roof. His sore knee jostled against the wood. He ground his teeth together to keep from wailing.

Most of his body was atop the cabin. Only his sore leg hung over the edge. He grabbed it with both hands and yanked it onto the roof. The lights to his room flashed on a moment later.

Bobby could hear her below him, inspecting his room. Dread filled him when he remembered he'd left Wesley's briefcase open. He recited again and again that she would think Wesley had left it open. It didn't help much. To take his mind off things, he massaged his sore knee while he waited.

"Clear," Regina finally stated.

The tension melted from Bobby's body. They would have his rifles in a few moments, but for now he could relax. Aside from all the lights turned on in the house, it was pitch-black out here. As long as they didn't think to check the roof, he'd be safe. He could take his time waiting for them to fall asleep. Then he'd climb down the tree and slip away into the night. Even his knee was starting to feel better now that he was at ease.

"Kerry, Wesley, go join her," Decker instructed. "Kerry, you wait at the top of the stairs. You'll be in my line of vision the whole time. Wesley, wait at the bottom so you can always keep an eye on Regina. Regina, get to the gun case. There's probably ammo kept nearby."

There was no argument. It may've been Brady's plan to come here, but Decker had slid smoothly into the position of de facto leader.

Bobby peered over the edge of the roof. He'd never climbed down from the top of the house before. It looked manageable, even with his swollen knee.

"Kerry, where are you—?"

"I'm fine," Kerry cut Decker off as her head popped out of Bobby's window. "There's a tree outside this open window. Maybe that's how the murderer got in and out."

Kerry didn't pull her head back in. She kept examining the tree and the ground below.

She's a sentinel trained to kill you.

"We've got the guns!" Wesley exclaimed excitedly.

A pair of footsteps raced up the stairs, while Bobby could make out ammunition sliding into the chamber. The fool had abandoned Regina below. The thought that a killer might still be loose in the house had vanished from Wesley's mind.

Bobby held his breath to eliminate the risk of Kerry hearing. Her head continued to swivel back and forth, searching through the darkness. He was afraid to pull his head back over the ledge. Now that they were armed, he needed to avoid attracting their attention.

"Thanks for waiting," Regina said dryly as she trudged up the stairs.

Blood was rushing to Bobby's head as he waited for Kerry to recede back into the house. Her patience to observe the surroundings, and the mechanical way she surveyed the area, was uncanny. He demanded to know what happened to the girl who ran away screaming at the sight of a rat.

She's a trybaby.

"Whatever, you're fine," Wesley dismissed Regina's barb. "We got that motherfucker now. Decker, get ready to open that door!" he commanded as though he was in charge. "We're going to blast whatever's on the other side."

Wesley was brimming with confidence now that they had weapons. Bobby wondered how much Wesley would be panicking right now if there weren't any bullets.

"No need," Decker said. Calm as ever.

That caught Kerry's attention. Her head swooped back into the house, and footsteps cut through the bedroom toward Decker. "What do you *mean* there's no need?"

Regina had reached the top of the stairs and marched down the hall. As far as Bobby could tell, they were all outside the bathroom.

Now's my chance, Bobby thought. I can disappear into the night until I reach a neighbor.

"If we've got him cornered," Decker explained. "Let's just call the sheriff."

Bobby scrapped his plans to escape. They might not know who he was, but Knotts did. If Knotts arrived to find two bodies, Bobby would be his first suspect. He'd reconsider his belief that Bobby was gone for the weekend, and tear the place apart looking for him.

Knotts knows the area, too. He'll know all the places you're likely to run and hide. He'd sick the dogs on you if it didn't deprive him the fun of hunting you down himself. Maybe he'll even use Decker's blade on you.

I'll just never file a police report. I swear.

Do you think Knotts'll believe he can trust a simpleton like you to keep quiet?

Bobby grabbed his forehead, hoping they'd act as tourniquets to all the negativity. His inner demons continued to press the issue.

Besides orchestrating this, that's his role in this heist. To cover it up. Think this is the first robbery

Knotts' staged? How many other crime scenes do you think he's "massaged" to rid any signs of his involvement?

I need my pills.

How easy do you think it'd be for Knotts to make your death look like a suicide?

Just need my pills.

Bobby practically leapt to the tree. He hated having to climb down the trunk slowly to cut down on the noise. Every precious second mattered.

The chance to run away until they were gone had passed. Two of them were dead, and now they were calling their ringleader. Folks around town would wonder why they were in Bobby's home to begin with, but Knotts had already come up with a plausible story of them booking his house for a vacation on one of the home-sharing Internet sites. People already trusted Knotts. Couple that with the two corpses, and that Bobby still hadn't taken his prescription meds, and the town would be willing to believe whatever story Knotts fed them.

Bobby couldn't allow them to contact Knotts. If the sheriff had time to get his version of what happened out to the public first, it wouldn't matter who Bobby told the truth to.

"I'll go call . . . ." Wesley started off eagerly before his
voice trailed off.

Kerry groaned. "Stay here with them if you're worried the killer might *not* be trapped in the bathroom but waiting downstairs for you. *I'll* go alone."

"Regina, give her the knife," Decker instructed.

Bobby swung around the tree as Kerry reached the stairs. He was grateful she was unaware of the phone in Pop's study. When he heard her reach the living room before he was out of the tree, he knew he had no other option.

"Did you guys hear something outside?" Decker asked from above.

The drop hurt worse than he'd expected, leaving him to hobble around the house to the utility box. He couldn't make out which circuit controlled the power to the living room in the darkness.

"It's a weird phone," Wesley shouted down to Kerry, obviously terrified she didn't know how to call for help.

"I've made calls on one before," she assured him.

Bobby had hoped the rotary phone would prove to be an enigma to her, but she handled it like a veteran. He was once again left with no other choice.

The screaming started immediately.

16

"Kerry! Are you okay down there?" Decker shouted down to her. His voice boomed, but he still sounded in control.

"I'm—"

"*Did you make the call?*" Wesley's voice cracked as he shrieked. He'd been the loudest when Bobby cut the power and all the lights went out.

"—fine," Kerry continued in a seething voice. "No. I had one last number to dial before the call could go through."

"Useless bitch," Wesley muttered, loud enough for Bobby to hear.

Something scratched across the top floor. "Follow me," Decker said, before calling out, "Kerry, don't move. We'll be down in a moment."

A moment later, from his hiding spot behind a tree, Bobby watched a slight glow pass by Pop's study, then his own room. It wasn't hard to pick out against the empty backdrop of night.

That Decker is prepared for *everything*. Bet the light is just for their benefit. He can probably see in the dark.

That's why you should run now, while he's still got to babysit them.

The glimmer started to dim as it reached his room. "*It's going out!*" Wesley cried.

"Calm down, I've got plenty more matches," Decker replied. A moment later, the radiance was as strong as ever.

Running would get Bobby nowhere. He'd cut them off from calling Knotts, but he was still in the same dilemma. If they were allowed to leave, word would get back to the sheriff about what happened. He didn't need much of an imagination to believe Knotts wouldn't want his involvement in the horrors of tonight to blow up in a massive scandal. Bobby didn't trust he'd ever be safe again.

There is one *way to ensure they never leave and talk to Knotts. You've already* killed *two of them.*

Bobby pushed the voice down as far as it would go. Despite the two fatalities, they were accidents. He wasn't a murderer, and he wasn't going to become one now.

But I can't run.

You can't just stay here, either.

"Some place you picked here," Regina needled Wesley as they tramped downstairs. "Doesn't even have a reliable power source."

Wesley opened his mouth to protest, but Decker cut him off. "It was no accident the power went out when it did."

"You mean, the killer—"

"Yes," Decker stated bluntly. "I heard something rustling outside by the house right before the lights went out. This maniac's been close enough to hear our conversations. That's how he knew exactly when to stop us from calling the sheriff."

Bobby counted himself lucky that Decker had chosen to play their guardian. He didn't want to think about how short a pursuit would last if Decker ever decided to search for him.

"I don't like being alone in the dark with some crazy on the loose," Wesley said, his voice trembling.

There was another scratch, and the light made its way to the fireplace. A few logs kept nearby were thrown onto the hearthstone.

"See if there's some paper lying around to start a fire with," Decker said.

As they fumbled around inside searching for kindling, Bobby took the time to tackle his quandary. He had to get the state police to show up and arrest the intruders before his guests could contact Knotts. Decker and Regina appeared to be hardened criminals, but if Wesley or Kerry were facing charges, he imagined they'd implicate the sheriff immediately if it meant reducing their sentences. Then it wouldn't matter that he hadn't taken his pills yet.

He hoped the corpses wouldn't matter, either.

Wesley breathed a sigh of relief as a fire roared to life. "We should see if there are any candles lying around," Regina suggested. "I don't want to be trapped in this room until dawn."

"We should *go*," Kerry stated.

Bobby's skin coated itself in a thin sweat as his eyes shot to the van. Cutting the power to the house had done nothing but pushed them closer to leaving. Once they departed, he had no way of stopping them from communicating with Knotts.

You could strand them here by stealing their van.

The thought was appealing. He doubted they'd flee the house while it was pitch-black out. Not with two of them already dead. They'd practically be giftwrapped for the state police.

I don't have the keys.

"Can you see the van from here?" Decker asked. "Me, neither. And I don't like stomping through the woods, calling attention to myself stepping on branches, in the dark, with a murderer on the loose."

Bobby couldn't allow himself to relax. Their escape may have been halted for now, but the sun would come up eventually. The van wasn't the only thing that would become exposed in the daylight. Now that they knew he was close by, it would be much harder to hide.

"Isn't there a flashlight?" Regina asked.

If they even waited for morning. They sounded determined to get to Knotts.

"I dropped it in the basement," Kerry confessed.

"Stupid bitch," Wesley muttered loud enough to be heard again.

Bobby debated letting the air out of the tires, deciding against it. Wesley was scared enough that he'd hound them to keep driving on the rims until they were out of the woods. He'd probably coax them with money if they ushered him to safety.

"Call me a bitch again," Kerry challenged him.

"W-well," Wesley stammered after a long pause. The brat had probably never been spoken to that way, and couldn't let it go without responding. "You left it below. *You* should be the one to go get it."

"No one's going into the basement," Decker barked. "No one's splitting up—"

"We did it a few minutes ago!" Wesley whined.

"When we had electricity and could see each other!" Regina pointed out the obvious.

"We're staying right here until we've figured out what to do next," Decker continued as if he'd never been interrupted.

A gentle wind breezed through the trees, cooling the perspiration matted on Bobby's skin. The intruders shuddered inside at the slight chill. In case they'd missed the gust, the flames flickered at its touch.

"The windows," Kerry rasped. There was a yelp inside. Bobby was sure it was Wesley.

"I don't like the idea of whoever's out there having so many ways of getting in," Regina observed.

The logs scraped against each other, and a moment later, the glow had grown, then multiplied as it spread to the kitchen. One of them had grabbed a piece of firewood to bear as a torch as they made their way about the first floor of the cabin and one by one, the windows on the bottom floor were yanked shut.

Bobby didn't move from his hiding spot until he was sure the first floor was sealed shut, and the flame returned to the fireplace. He then slunk across the ground until he sidled up along one of the closed windows.

"What about the upstairs windows?" Wesley asked. His voice was muffled through the pane, but Bobby could make out it was still panicked.

"We won't be staying long," Decker informed him.

Bobby grew tense at the announcement, stealing a glance at the van. They intended to get away in the night.

"Do we just bolt for the van?" Kerry asked.

They would escape if they did. He'd only been able to sneak up on Misty, and it'd helped that she'd been high. There was no way he'd gain the element of surprise if they ran.

Decker must've shaken his head.

"Why not?" Wesley asked, flustered.

"Whoever's out there is cunning," Decker explained. Bobby had to keep from laughing. If only all my teachers could hear that, he thought. "He got inside without any of us knowing and picked Misty off. That doesn't mean he isn't armed. If we go charging out of here, we might turn into ducks marching ourselves into one of those carnival shooting galleries."

Bobby wanted to believe Decker was just as afraid as the rest of them, but his voice said otherwise. Decker wasn't fearful, just cautious. He didn't know what he was up against, so he wasn't taking any unnecessary chances getting them all out of there.

It made Bobby uneasy how clearly Decker was still thinking. He worried that the longer Decker assessed the situation, the more likely he was to figure out Bobby was just a scared little boy hiding in the dark.

Alone. And unarmed.

"If we're not racing out of here and we're not staying, what *are* we doing?" Kerry asked, exasperated.

There was a long pause in the conversation. Bobby thought it could only be brought about by one of two things. The first was that they had no idea what to do. But that didn't sound like Decker.

"*No*! That's *suicide*!" Regina protested a moment later. She was clearly reacting to something, which confirmed Bobby's suspicion. Decker had whispered the plan to them.

He thinks I'm close enough to overhear them.

Bobby risked a quick peek through the window during another pause, and saw the tops of four heads clustered together, bobbing when they spoke. He ducked his head back from the window when they broke from the huddle.

They're plotting something sinister. They don't want you to hear because they want it to snare you.

"Start loading the rifles," Decker commanded. The other three sprang into action. Wesley flew to Pop's rifle case, passing them out. Kerry counted out the three boxes of ammo that Pop had kept close to the display, and made sure everyone had one. Decker then instructed them on how to properly line up their shots using the sights on the barrel, and to aim at the chest of their intended target because it gave them a higher margin for error.

"I won't let you down," Regina protested. "I've been keeping up with my running even after my expulsion. I'll get there quick."

Bobby's stomach curdled. He tried to come up with a plan to keep them from leaving. There were all the tools he'd left lying around during the day. He could slash the tires and puncture the gas tank. That would keep them from getting to Knotts.

If he had enough time. His window to find those tools in the dark and sabotage the car had closed, especially if Regina raced to the van.

"I know you will. But I've got to do my part first," Decker replied.

Bobby was left to wonder what had been said in that lengthy conversation.

They've got something evil schemed for you.

"Do you think your plan will work?" Wesley asked, his voice quaking worse than ever.

There was a hiss from Kerry to be quiet.

"I do," Decker insisted over Kerry's rasps. "It's my plan. I can't ask any of you to take the risk for me. I've got to be the one to do it since I'm the only one who knows how to hotwire a vehicle . . . even if it means . . . 'walking the plank.'

"The van should be parked about twenty yards in front of the front door. When I step out into the darkness, I'm going to walk in a straight line. Keep the rifles pointed where you saw me last. If you hear *any* sign of struggle, open fire. When I get to the van, I'm going to turn on the headlights."

Bobby followed the logic of Decker's plan. The intruders believed he was more dangerous than they were, and needed to retreat back to their ringleader.

Decker didn't know what he was up against, but knew risks were going to be necessary to escape. Walking through the dark seemed crazy, but using something to light the way would be suicide if their enemy had a gun. Decker was choosing to go alone in the dark so that he'd be tougher to spot, and if he was attacked, the rest of the group would not only be safe, but the killer would have revealed his position.

Something still seemed amiss. Decker had taken the time to whisper to the intruders as they conspired to come up with a plan. Yet now they were talking openly about its execution.

Are they still concerned about me overhearing them or not?

"I got the door," Kerry's muffled voice announced. "You ready?"

"Ready," Decker confirmed. "Open it on three."

Bobby shifted his eyes to the van. Decker's plan could turn into a stroke of luck. He could lie in wait by the van if he beat Decker to it, then get the drop on him. He then wouldn't need the keys to steal their ride and could maroon them in the house they were robbing until the cops arrived.

"One," Kerry announced.

Bobby didn't stick around. He had to get to the van before Decker did. The front door opened before he made it halfway.

He halted, waiting. Footsteps trudged out into the open. Bobby could just make out a silhouette by the front door before it was swallowed up in the darkness. He was pretty sure it was carrying a gun.

Decker kept a brisk pace. Bobby had gone out wide from the house to avoid the chance that Decker would spot him as they both advanced on the van. Bobby started toward the ride again, freezing at the snapping of a twig beneath his foot.

The other footsteps stopped abruptly, too. Bobby stared ahead to where he'd last heard them, sure that Decker was glaring back at him.

Don't move. Don't even quiver. He'll hear you.

My skin's crawling. I can feel his eyes on me.

He knows where you are. He sees you clear as day. He can peer deep into your soul. He's got Pop's rifle aimed right between your eyes.

Far off, the brusque stride began again. Lights went on in the van as the door opened, and the headlights shot out across the woods. Bobby hobbled closer to the van. Even if Decker heard him, there'd be no way to discern that it wasn't just some woodland critter startled into hiding from the sudden lights. The engine roared to life a moment later.

Bobby hid behind a tree ten yards in front of the van. He'd dismissed his farfetched notions of sneaking up on Decker. He'd have to cross in front of the headlights to get to the man, and pry him out of the van without him fighting back. He was beside himself, grieving that they were going to get away.

The driver's door popped open. "We're good to go, guys," Decker inexplicably called back to the house. Then he did something even more outrageous. The door slammed, and a figure passed in front of the lights.

He's heading back inside.

Bobby skulked toward the van, never taking his eyes off Decker. It was incredulous that someone so thoughtful would make such a blunder. He didn't question it. People made mistakes all the time under duress, and Bobby was more than happy to capitalize on the blunder of others. Especially from someone as ruthless as Decker.

It wasn't until he opened the van door that he realized the true blunder was his own. The van's interior lights turned on.

"*He's in the van!*" Kerry screamed before the vehicle was bombarded with bullets.

The van rocked as a bullet slammed into it. Bobby lost his balance and slipped to his knees. It may have saved his life as the next moment, a second round whizzed through the passenger window's Plexiglas where his head had been. He felt it breeze over his hair as it flew by. Bobby ducked himself lower as the next shot shattered the pane.

Two more shots thudded against the van's door. One tore the upholstery of the driver's headrest. He dove low to the ground, until another shot ricocheted off the gas tank. The smell of fuel irritated his nostrils as the ground around him grew damp.

The shots kept coming. They had to have loaded every rifle in Pop's display. Air whooshed out of the tire as the front of the van collapsed to the ground. One shot sailed high, hitting the tree behind him. He shielded himself as singed bark hailed down on his back.

Bobby had no time to ask how many shots that'd been. Another rang out, hitting the interior lights. Sparks flew everywhere. He crawled away until his palms no longer felt the puddles of fuel.

Shots followed him as he retreated. He could see his leg was caught in the light, and crawled back behind the van. His hands and knees splashed through the lake of gas. They must've seen the movement.

The gunfire shadowed him. The dashboard lights flickered on and off as the next shot hit it. They continued to riddle the van with bullets, punching holes through it. One of them collided with metal, sending debris flying toward Bobby. He shrieked as something stung the back of his hand, fearing he'd been hit. The debris continued to roll up his arm until it struck him in the chin, and then plopped down in front of him. Bobby stopped screaming long enough to see it had been one of the van's door handles that had struck him. His wails drew the firing squad's attention. Bobby had to duck his head low as the next two shots sailed over it. His head popped up at the sound of something ricocheting around the van's interior, and saw they had hit the rearview mirror.

Another of the windows was shot out as the bullet flew into one of the trees behind him. Bark bit at his back. The lights in the dashboard died when another projectile hit it.

What're they thinking? The neighbors'll wonder what's going on.

No. They won't. The neighbors will just think it's the Boyle brothers setting off fireworks again and go back to sleep.

Bobby curled himself into a ball, waiting for the thundering to stop. He was inhaling gas fumes and couldn't stop coughing. Not that they could hear him over the blasts. The van's engine began to smoke, drawing two more shots. The headlights shattered and died. Sparks landed nearby. Bobby was sure one of them would hit the ocean of gas surrounding the van.

The gunfire probably stopped sooner than Bobby thought. It was tough to tell, as shots kept echoing through his head.

"Regina!" Decker howled in the intermission. "*Now!*"

17

Bobby caught the sounds Regina made dashing through the woods before the bullets started flying again. Tufts of dirt flew into his face as their shots closed in around him.

Now that he was caught in it, Bobby could see Decker's full plan. It was masterfully conceived and executed.

Decker had suspected that Bobby had still been close by, listening in, and had used that to his advantage. When he'd announced his intentions to head to the van in the dark, that had been a ruse to bait Bobby, either into attacking Decker on his way to the van, or sneaking into the van when Decker left it running and unoccupied. The real plan had been what Bobby hadn't heard, when Decker dropped his voice to a whisper: Once Bobby revealed his position, they were to open fire. Decker had been willing to put his life on the line. He'd informed them he'd walk in a straight line to the van, and if they heard any sign of struggle, to fire in that direction. If Bobby had chosen to strike, there was a good chance they would've hit him. Failing to draw Bobby out in the walk to the vehicle, the van itself would then serve as an alluring trap, abandoned and running. And it worked. They had clearly kept their eyes peeled for the van's lights coming on.

The plan hadn't merely been to lure Bobby out of hiding, but to get help. Not having Regina run to the van should've set off alarms in Bobby's head, especially when she'd promised not to let Decker down, but his brain proved to be as useless a lump as everyone suspected. Only now did he see what her speed was intended for. She had sprinted toward Mr. Harris' house.

Ha! He's not home.

They entered your *house when they thought you were gone. Why wouldn't they do the same with Mr. Harris?*

But what could they—

His *phone is working just fine.*

Two more shots punched holes through the side of the van. They no longer concerned him as much as Regina. Their frequency had died down, and he'd noticed their pattern of shots alternating between the engine, door, and back tire, with little regard to accuracy. He realized the intention was merely to keep him pinned behind the vehicle while Regina ran.

Bobby needed to stop her from calling for help. Knotts was sure to respond, and he'd bring all his deputies. With two bodies, and Bobby unmedicated, Knotts might be able to convince his subordinates to shoot to kill. Then he wouldn't have to worry about Bobby telling the truth.

He needed to get out from behind the van first. Bobby waited until another shot hit the smoking engine, then bolted toward Mr. Harris' house. His knee felt stiff and heavy. After getting into a rhythm, his running smoothed out, but he was still limping as he weaved through the trees.

Regina's head start was a problem. So was the pace he heard her run before they opened fire again. But he had an ace up his sleeve. Regina would most likely stick to the road between their houses. The long, winding road. She didn't know about the trail that cut through the trees to Mr. Harris'.

It was his one chance to make up ground.

He tripped over a root and came down hard on his bad knee. As he picked himself up, he noticed the gunfire had stopped. Bobby doubted it was because they'd run out of ammo. There was no time to worry about them finding out that he'd fled. He had bigger problems.

Mr. Harris' lights had just turned on.

Bobby shambled along through the woods, holding out hope that he could still stop her. He judged he only had about twenty yards to go to reach the front door.

The sight of the house up close brought a sense of déjà vu. He'd forgotten how closely Mr. Harris' cabin resembled his own. He recalled having the same feeling of similarity about the place while Pop had been building it for Mr. Harris. Sometimes, in the later stages of its construction, he'd confused it with their home. The only real difference he could recall was the fireplace. Whereas theirs used real wood, Mr. Harris had insisted on having an automatic gas starter put in.

Pop had had a good laugh about that one. "Guy wants to feel like he's got a place out in the country, but doesn't want to abandon all the amenities of his soft city life." Pop's cackle echoed through Bobby's memory. "If he had to actually get his hands dirty living the country life, he'd be reduced to a real crybaby in seconds."

Bobby had hoped Regina would stumble around in the dark, trying to familiarize herself with the house, giving him more time to close in on her. Lights popped on every few seconds as she lit the place up. He'd forgotten the power would be working here. If she could see where she was going, she'd be able to find a phone in no time.

The front door had been busted open. Bobby didn't think it would shut properly anymore until it was replaced.

Mr. Harris isn't going to like coming back to a broken door. Especially since he probably keeps a key under the welcome mat, just like we do.

Out of curiosity, he stooped down, lifted the doormat, and smirked. Mr. Harris had copied practically everything else in their layout. It shouldn't have surprised Bobby that Mr. Harris had mimicked the location of their spare key, too.

You've got more important things to worry about.

Bobby seized his good luck that Regina had her back to him and slid in quietly through the busted door.

". . . been attacked. He's already *killed* two of my friends!"

She's already called the sheriff!

Fool! You should've ripped the power from the circuit breaker again.

Then she'd know I was near.

But Knotts *wouldn't know* anything!

It was too late to reverse his decision now. It was too late to keep Knotts from finding out he was interfering with the break-in. Even if he hung up the phone on Regina, the sheriff's office traced every call that came in. At the very least, a deputy would come to investigate. Bobby didn't believe Knotts would let a deputy handle this situation. He knew the sheriff would arrive personally to clean up the mess.

Bobby saw he still had a chance to turn this around. Knotts wouldn't be able to spread his version of the truth around town if he was busy taking care of Bobby and the crime scene to fit his narrative. For whatever reason, Knotts had believed Bobby wouldn't be home this weekend, and had fed the intruders the story that they had rented the house from Bobby, in case any neighbors had stopped by while they were robbing the place. But if Bobby refuted that claim, and there was no evidence they'd ever contacted him, their story would fall apart. He still expected them to roll on Knotts if they were facing jail time.

For all that to happen, they needed to be caught in their lie. Now that Regina had called the sheriff's department, the option to run to the state police first was long gone. He now not only needed to face the intruders head on, he needed to apprehend them. And Knotts. Only then could he go to the state police. When his captives spilled their story without anything to back it up, he was positive it wouldn't matter he was well past taking his meds, and would be vindicated for the siblings he'd accidentally killed.

"Three seventy-four Lakeview Drive," Regina answered into the phone.

She seemed completely unaware of his presence as he tiptoed closer. Bobby looked for something blunt to strike her with. He didn't want a repeat of what happened with Brady and Misty, but he felt she wouldn't go down easy unless he really walloped her. She wouldn't appreciate a massive headache and a giant lump on the back of her skull, but she'd live.

His eyes skimmed across the room to the fireplace. He delicately removed a poker from its cast-iron holder.

"Wait. . . . What? No. I *came* from there," Regina said into the receiver.

Bobby nearly snorted. The fool had given the dispatcher this address and was now trying to argue with them. He held out hope there *would* be a chance he could restrain all four of them before Knotts arrived.

"What?" she gasped incredulously into the phone. "Oh, god. . . ." Her voice trailed off, and she gave a loud sniff.

Had Bobby been on the other side of the room, he would've been convinced the sniveling had merely been an attempt to hold her emotions in check. Her voice sounded distraught enough. However, being within arm's reach of Regina, he detected something in her reaction to the snuffle.

Recognition.

She smells the gas on your hands and knees!

Regina wasted no time in whirling around at him. Bobby had just enough time to throw his arms up to defend his throat from the knife. The blade Decker had given her slashed across the back of his right hand. The gas stung his cut immediately.

Bobby barely had time to shriek. She swung the knife wildly at him again and again. Each time he retreated just out of her reach, watching specks of his own blood fly from the tip of the damp blade.

"*Miss? Are you still there? Hello?*" the confused dispatcher asked through the abandoned phone receiver.

He nearly tripped backing into the hearthstone surrounding the fireplace. She looked at him with the eyes of a cat spotting a cornered mouse. It was sickening watching her face light up so gleefully.

Don't just watch it, fool, defend *yourself!*

Bobby swung the poker at the incoming blade. He missed, but connected with Regina's wrist, deflecting her aim from his chest. The blow weakened her grip on the hilt, and sent the knife flying across the room.

He brandished the poker, hoping for a quick surrender now that he was the only one armed. Regina called his bluff.

Her hands clutched the poker and attempted to wrench it from his grasp. Bobby grabbed the tip of it with his other hand. He was already having difficulty squeezing the poker with his slashed hand. The blood oozing out of his wound onto his palm made it tough to grip, too.

"*Miss!*" the dispatcher called through the line.

The two wrestled for control of the poker. Bobby's size had usually given him an edge in any tug of war, but now that he was face-to-face with Regina, he saw she matched him in build. It was also apparent that the loss of her scholarship hadn't deterred her from keeping up with her training. Not only was she of equal stature, she looked chiseled from marble; he was barely holding on each time she tried to rip the poker from his hands.

The constant tugs were jarring to his sore ribs. Bobby favored his side with each jerk. The advantage was obvious to both of them, and Regina seized it, releasing one hand from the poker to claw at his face. A moment later, blood blinded one of his eyes.

While blinking the red from his pupils, Regina changed tactics, charging forward and knocked him off balance; he collided with the wall behind him. The poker crashed into his throat, closing off his windpipe.

His legs gave out on him, and Regina let him drop to all fours. Bobby relinquished the poker as soon as she gave it a gentle tug. Once she had it, she brought it down on his spine. He tried to shriek, but his lungs were too busy trying to draw their next breath.

"*Miss!*"

Bobby curled into a ball, preparing himself for a thrashing that never came. In its place, he heard the sound of a nozzle being turned.

Regina grabbed him by the hair, yanking him to his knees. Bobby attempted to flee when he saw she'd already started the fire. The poker came down hard just under his left shoulder blade, dropping him back to the ground. He was jerked upward again, this time with the poker across his neck.

"*Are you all right?*" the dispatcher's voice called out from the other side of the room.

Bobby had trouble deciding which problem to tackle first. Regina was using the poker to choke the life out of him. With his hands occupied trying to pry the bar from his neck, she was also leaning on him, forcing him toward the flame.

He threw one hand from the poker to the hearthstone to keep himself at arm's length from the fire. The poker squeezed tighter against his throat as Regina wasted no time seizing her advantage. His knees started to wobble. Regina picked up on that as well, shifting more of her weight against him, forcing him closer to the blaze.

Something dripped off the sliced hand Bobby was using to prop himself against the hearthstone. It became engulfed in flames too quickly to be perspiration or blood.

The gas is still on my hands.

She's gonna cook you alive.

"Miss! If you're still there, stay on the line! I'm calling the sheriff!"

Bobby snapped his head back, connecting with the bridge of her nose.

"Muddafugga!" she managed to get out.

He felt he'd broken her nose, but there was no time to celebrate. Bobby gasped for air as the pressure against his neck subsided, then pushed off from the wall as hard as he could, launching them both backward.

Regina recovered quicker than he would've believed. He gave the poker a tug, disappointed to find he couldn't free it from her grasp, then feeling it tighten around his throat a moment later. She had regained her footing, no longer being driven backward by his backpedaling, and threw a knee into the back of his thigh. He lost his balance, but the poker around his neck kept his knees from reaching the ground. For a moment, he got to experience a hanging firsthand.

She pushed forward toward the fireplace again. Bobby barely found his footing along the way. His hands groped feebly at hers, hoping to loosen her ironclad grip on the rod across his neck.

"*Please pick up, Sheriff. Please pick up.*"

Their momentum picked up. Bobby's feet couldn't keep up, stumbling over each other. He involuntarily dove headfirst into the hearthstone.

Regina tripped over him as he toppled to the ground. She let go of the poker as she tried to brace herself for the impact.

"*Cheryl? Why in god's name are you calling me at—*what *time does that clock sa—*"

Bobby feared his neck was broken. His forehead felt cool and damp. When he opened his eyes, he was greeted with the sight of his own blood staining Mr. Harris' floor. The sickening thud of his skull striking the corner of the hearthstone echoed in his ears.

"*Hank, listen to me,*" the dispatcher pleaded from the phone receiver. The voice sounded like it was coming from the other side of the galaxy.

Bobby wiggled his fingers, relieved they could move. His limbs felt stiff, but as he tested them, he found them all to be operational.

"*Cheryl? What is it?*"

That's Knotts' voice!

You're gonna need *those limbs now. You better start running fast as you can. Give yourself the biggest head start, cause once Knotts gets here—*

"*I've got a woman on the line,*" the dispatcher explained, "*calling from Mr. Harris' place. Says she and her friends were attacked by some madman. She says the rest are still back at the cabin they've been attacked in, but the address she gave me is also Mr. Harris'."*

"*Cheryl? Cheryl? I can't hear you. Cheryl?*" Knotts shouted through the connection.

"*I'm here, Hank.*"

"*I can't make out what . . . . Cheryl! Where's that screaming coming from?*"

Regina was wailing like a banshee as she pried her head from the fireplace. Her frantic pupils bounced around the top of her eyeballs, trying to get a glimpse of the flames that were gorging themselves on the top of her skull.

She beat her hands against her head in a desperate effort to extinguish the blazes. Regina didn't appear to notice that her right hand hung limply at her wrist. Bobby believed she'd shattered it when crashing against the unforgiving hearthstone. Her hands burst into flames the moment she struck them against her head.

The gas! Oh, god, she's got gas on them where I touched her.

"*Oh, my god. Oh, my god, Hank! She's dying! I'm listening to her dying!*" Cheryl shrieked through the receiver.

Bobby rolled out of the way as Regina ran from the fireplace. Her screech was more than enough incentive not to be set ablaze as well. He witnessed firsthand just how magnificent the former track athlete's speed had been as she raced around the living room, trying to outrun the fire. Bobby had to look away each time she ran toward him. Her screaming face grew more horrifying the more it was swallowed in flames.

"*She's dying, Hank! She's dying! She's—*"

Cheryl's voice cut off as Regina tripped over the phone cord, severing the line. Regina sprang to her feet in no time and continued her mad dash to flee from her agony.

A decapitated chicken ran with more grace.

As Regina tumbled over a couch, Bobby noticed the trail of flames she was leaving. Snapping his neck around the room, he saw the curtains, couch, and portraits hanging on the walls had already caught fire. They roared at him, convincing him to get out while he still could.

Bobby barely kept his balance as he staggered to his feet. His neck was sore, and the change in elevation stung the gash in his forehead where he'd slammed into the hearthstone. A fresh wave of blood gushed down his face.

Regina's rise to her feet was less steady this time. Her sprints around the room had been reduced to lurches that zigged and zagged depending on which foot took the next step. Her cries had gone through the greatest metamorphosis. They were merely hisses that rattled around her throat.

A throat that had clearly been burned to a crisp.

Bobby hobbled toward the door, doing his best to ignore Regina's death rattle. He halted in his tracks when he saw someone standing outside, barring his escape.

The tear-filled eyes didn't fool him. He knew he was finally standing face-to-face with Decker.

18

Bobby didn't see the rifle until Decker raised it. For once in his life, he reacted quickly. He dove to his right, out of the view of the doorway, as Decker fired off a round. A lamp by Mr. Harris' sofa went flying into the growing wall of flames.

Pop would be proud that you finally learned to think on your feet.

That maniac wouldn't follow me into a burning house, would he?

I'm sure he'll be satisfied listening to you burn alive.

Regina stamped a few more times, refusing to go down. The blazes that had engulfed her head had spread down to her shoulders. The first thought that came to Bobby was that her brain had to have melted, but she still staggered forward.

"*Regina!*" Decker cried from the doorway. "I'm sorry. I *love* you."

A moment later, another shot rang out. Regina's body tumbled backward. She didn't get up this time. Her body didn't even stir after she hit the floor.

Gotta get outta here. I'm gonna be well done if I stay too much longer.

You'd deserve it. Three dead now because of you.

They weren't . . . . *None* of them were my fault!

His head felt so hot he thought it'd caught fire. He stayed low to the ground, finding the heat slightly more bearable, and crawled on his hands and knees to the nearest window, making sure to keep them as far from the flames as possible.

The feat became more impossible by the second.

His whole body felt tired by the time he climbed the wall to open the window. Decker was already waiting for him. Tears streaked down Decker's face, but Bobby could clearly see the wild look in his eyes.

You finally get to see what Decker looks like unhinged.

Bobby ducked his head as Decker aimed the rifle and squeezed off another round. The window shattered, raining glass down on Bobby. If any of the shards cut him, he didn't notice. His body had too many other cuts and bruises to deal with.

The air was thick with smoke, but he could barely hear himself choke over the roaring flames. Bobby had to get out of the house fast, but if Decker was waiting for him again, he was dead. He knew his next attempt at escape had to succeed.

Bobby popped his head up through the window. When Decker set his sights on him again, Bobby made as if to run back toward the front door, before crouching back to the floor. The drop may have been involuntary. The combination of the smoke and inferno nearly knocked him out.

A bullet sailed through the window overhead. He couldn't hear if Decker had run back toward the front door over the rumble of the fire. He couldn't worry about that now. Bobby set his sights deeper into the bowels of the house. Where the living room met the kitchen. Where Pop had built a door leading to the basement.

Oh, I hope it's cooler in the cellar.

Just rest a little while longer up here. It's not so bad. You won't even notice when your liquefied eyeballs spill out of their sockets.

He pushed down the tempting thoughts, willing himself to keep crawling. Every time he thought of quitting (and the thought crept into his mind every second) he forced himself to hear Pop's voice.

Challenging him. Berating him. But always urging him to press on.

Bobby bumped his head against the cellar door. The smoke had gotten so thick he couldn't see the end of his nose. His arms felt so heavy, he had trouble lifting them to the doorknob.

Just give up. Decker didn't take the bait anyway. He's not waiting for you to emerge from the front door. He knows you're trying to escape through the cellar door. Decker's aiming Pop's gun at the door, just waiting for your head to poke out of it so he can blow it off. You're just making your last moments that much more excruciating.

Don't . . . li-listen. . . .

His fingers grazed the knob. He could barely squeeze his fingers around the handle, and the yank he gave was lifeless.

Just a little longer. Burning alive won't be so bad.

Keep . . . go . . . ing. . . .

You'll lose consciousness before your brain explodes from the heat.

Don't . . . quit. . . .

You won't feel your body burn to a crisp.

Don't be . . . a crybaby. . . .

I need my meds.

Be a trybaby.

The cold air across his face woke him up. He was facing down the steps leading into the cellar. Toward his salvation. His arm sank to the floor as soon as he let go of the doorknob. His body was so worn by the heat he had to slither down the steps.

He reached for the lower wooden planks that made up the stairs and dragged himself deeper into the basement. His feet took longer to get involved. They had cramped up being in the scorching inferno for that long.

The flames seemed aware they were in a race. He could see them out of the corner of his eyes, chasing him down the stairs, devouring the wooden railings. Fearful that the fire would consume him if he rose from the ground, Bobby frantically pulled himself down the steps. He didn't dare turn to see the giant mouth of flames pursuing him.

Bobby winced as he kicked off from one of the steps with his bad knee, launching himself forward. As uncomfortable as it felt, it was preferable to being swallowed by the blaze. He grit his teeth as he pulled away from the flames above.

When he reached the bottom of the stairs, he rose shakily to his feet, his aggravated knee fighting him as he put weight on it. He bore the agony as he hobbled across the cellar to the stairs leading outside.

Bobby didn't hesitate, bursting through the cellar door. If Decker was waiting there, so be it. A gunshot to the head would end his suffering quickly.

Nobody was waiting for him as he charged through the door. He tripped over the last step and he tumbled up and away from the burning cabin. The fresh, cool air tackled his throat. He gasped greedily for it. Bobby dropped down on all fours as his lungs aggressively tried to rid themselves of all the smoke he'd inhaled inside. He threw up more than once.

Quiet! Decker'll hear all the noise you're making.
Nobody can hear anything over that fire.

Mr. Harris' whole cabin was engulfed in flames. The height of the fire had grown taller than some of the nearby trees.

Bobby rolled into a sitting position to massage his legs. A cool wind swept across his back as it breezed toward the blaze. The wall of flames bent against the gust, sending some embers toward a nearby tree. He grimaced as he forced himself to rise. There was no time to sit and watch the house burn.

Knotts was coming. Regina's call had gotten through, and the dispatcher had summoned the sheriff. Even if Regina hadn't made the call, someone along the lake was going to notice the fire and report the emergency.

His objective was still the same. He needed to round up the surviving intruders before Knotts poked around to check their progress. Then he needed to get the drop on the sheriff. Everything would go smoothly as soon as he captured all of them. Their story wouldn't hold up under any scrutiny. The only thing the fire changed was now he had a deadline.

He had *some* time. Whether it was Knotts, or the fire department, they'd go to Mr. Harris' first. The firefighters would be doing their job, and the dispatcher had given Knotts Mr. Harris' address. Knotts or the firemen would also have to navigate through the long winding roads that Mr. Harris always detested, and avoided by driving along the lakeshore. That would slow them down even more, and give Bobby a little more time to deal with the intruders.

Bobby knew he'd have to be efficient with the little time he had. Regardless of whether Knotts or the firefighters were the first to respond, they wouldn't remain at Mr. Harris'. The blowing wind threatened to spread the fire. First responders would fan out to all the neighbors, instructing them they needed to evacuate their homes until the blaze was contained.

Firefighters knocking at his door would be the best case scenario, especially if he already had the intruders subdued and had retrieved his prescription from Misty. He wouldn't need to worry about trying to call the authorities if they arrived at his doorstep. Knotts couldn't shape the narrative of the botched heist if the intruders had already rolled on him to shave years off their sentences.

And if Knotts was the first to arrive?

Then you better hope you've got the survivors taken care of already.

His legs were stiff and wooden when he first started running, but loosened up as he gained some momentum. Aside from the drop in elevation every time he planted that foot on the ground, he didn't even notice the pain in his knee anymore.

Too many other wounds demanded his attention.

19

Racing footsteps scampered across the road. Bobby paused, aware that he wasn't alone. He waited until the running trailed off before starting up again. His legs groaned at the sudden changes in speed.

Decker's rushing back to them.

Bobby cut and weaved through the woods. Just like Regina, Decker was keeping to the winding road. Bobby pushed himself to run faster. He didn't believe he could restrain Kerry and Wesley before Decker arrived, but if he could intercept Decker, coming at him head on instead of behind, his biggest remaining obstacle would be neutralized. Unless he had to deal with Knotts. Bobby pushed that troubling thought down, not wanting to deal with the possibility until he had to.

A beam of light flashed through the windows of his house as he drew near, scouring the area. It swept toward the snap of a branch at the front of the house.

Kerry must've retrieved the flashlight from the cellar when they were convinced I'd gone after Regina.

"*Don't shoot!*" Decker shouted.

Bobby nixed any plan of ambushing Decker while he was alone in the dark. His target was already too close to the house, and the flashlight would make him an easy target to hit.

"*Where's Regina?*" Wesley's terrified voice called out as the front door flung open.

There was no time to bemoan the lost opportunity of subduing Decker while he was separated from the others. In his mind, he kept hearing the faint sounds of approaching sirens, and couldn't help but envision them surrounding his cabin.

They're not here yet. It's just my imagination.

It won't be for long.

"*She's . . .* gone," Decker replied, his voice losing strength. It sounded like he'd wept.

Bobby cut away from his house, giving it a wide berth. Whether Decker was with them or not, they were still armed. If he was going to take them on, he'd need to equip himself to fight. He had to assume they hadn't gone through all the rounds he'd kept in the house, although after shooting up the van, he didn't know how they'd have any ammunition left. They had the advantage in firepower, but he knew the layout of the house better.

He wished that improved his odds more significantly than it did.

His mind scrambled to patch a plan together. He'd left tools lying around his yard when he'd neglected his chores to enjoy some fishing, and had a rough idea of where everything lay. It wasn't ideal, bringing hammers and nails to a gunfight, but at least he'd have something that could pass for melee weapons.

The moonlight shimmered off the lake, guiding him as he charged down the slope. The illumination highlighted where Brady lay along the coast, the pickaxe still embedded in his shoulder.

The shore was so serene, it was hard to imagine all the chaos that had happened above. The only sound was from the waves splashing against the corpse.

And the faint wail of sirens in the distance.

He grabbed what he'd come for and began lugging it back up the slope. Bobby's trek was accompanied by the growing screams of sirens. He knew these were real.

You've got time. They've still got to make that long, weaving drive.

When he reached his backyard, he released his haul and caught his breath. His mind tried to work out who the siren belonged to: Knotts or firemen. At that distance he couldn't tell.

He berated himself for wasting time he didn't have before springing back into action. It was easy to remember where he'd left the hatchet and chainsaw. His fishing pole was where he'd dropped it. The screwdriver took a little searching around for, but when his hands skimmed over it, he shoved it in his pocket for future use. He knew precisely where the hammer and nails were, but gathering them was challenging because they were next to the cellar's exterior door. Bobby stalked toward the house as he made to retrieve them, slowing even further when he heard them inside.

"We don't have enough logs to keep this place lit 'til morning," Wesley cried, practically in tears.

"We've only got seven rounds left, too," Kerry updated them. There was a panicked gasp Bobby was sure came from Wesley. "Please. Can we just leave?"

The intensifying wails got Bobby moving again. It was comforting to hear they were scared. And running low on resources. But it wouldn't count for anything if he couldn't put his plan in motion.

"We . . . can't," Decker reluctantly confessed.

Bobby dragged what he'd collected from the shore along the side of the house his bedroom was on, leaving it there for later. He had to set up the rest of his scheme. Surprisingly, they gave no indication they'd heard him, which suited him just fine. They could be absorbed in their own conversation up to the moment he had them all bound and gagged.

"Why . . .?" Kerry started to ask, before her voice trailed off. "Because we shot up the van," she stated glumly.

Bobby was in the middle of unspooling his fishing line when he distinguished that the siren belonged to a firetruck. His lips unconsciously pursed themselves into a delighted smile that wasn't meant to last. In the distance, another alarm harmonized with the firetruck's.

Knotts!

"We've got no way out!" Wesley shrieked. "This is all *your* fucking fault, Decker! It was *your* plan. If you think *I'm* paying for the full amount of damages, you two've got another think coming. And fuck *Brady* for talking us into coming here. Him and his *big* plans."

"*First* off," Kerry rounded on him, "it was *your* aim that hit not only the engine, but one of the tires. Sec—"

"Calm down," Decker said, and the return of his composed tone froze Bobby momentarily. "Hear that?" he asked, and Bobby knew his sharp ears had picked up the sirens. "Help is on the way."

Bobby finished tying one end of the fishing line around the handle of the cellar door, and settled on taking the hammer with him. The nails would have to sit this one out. He feared they'd puncture him if he kept them in his pocket, and didn't want to hold them in case he had to grab one of them inside. With his decision made, he bolted toward the stump where he'd left the chainsaw and brought it closer to Pop's side of the house.

Knotts would show up at his front door, but the sheriff had to deal with the fire at Mr. Harris'. He *had* to. Bobby was sure of it. It was where the distress call had come from. As far as Knotts knew, that was where the issue with the burglary lay. Even when he pieced together something had gone wrong back at the house he was trying to rob, once the firefighters spotted him, he wouldn't be able to just leave the scene. Not without the first responders wondering why.

The firetruck was close enough where he could see the flashing lights whirling through the trees. Even through the narrow path with the tight turns, the truck was hauling ass to get to Mr. Harris' place. Bobby stood there, waiting for the sheriff's car.

The second set of flashing lights tore through the woods a moment later. Bobby's eyes trailed them as they drew near. He pressed himself for a backup plan in case Knotts pulled into his driveway, and came up empty.

Knotts is slowing down.

It's a sharp curve in front of our driveway. The firetruck did it, too, you just didn't pay attention because you knew they were going to Mr. Har—

He's coming to get you, Bobby.

The sheriff's vehicle had slowed down where the dirt path that was Bobby's driveway met the road. Bobby gave the chainsaw's cord a panicked jerk before he realized what he was doing. He flung his hands from the tool. The last thing he wanted was to betray his location to Knotts.

Keep going. Keep *going!*

Knotts' car was crawling along the road, but he hadn't stopped completely. The flashing lights were blinding and Bobby was sure the sheriff had spotted him next to the house.

Even if he sees me, he couldn't tell from there whether or not I'm one of the goons he sent.

Maybe, but the intruders inside can see you now, too. And they know you're not one of them.

The car inched along a little farther, then took off after the firetruck. Bobby hadn't even noticed he'd been holding his breath. Knotts had slowed down to make the tight turn after all, and he'd panicked for nothing.

"What! Where're they going! Where're they *going*?" Wesley squealed from the house.

Bobby chuckled mirthlessly. Decker was most likely explaining to him that they were responding to the fire. If only Decker was the one in hysterics.

He settled his hand back on the cord of the chainsaw. It was awkward gripping it while still holding the other end of the fishing line. He took a peek back at the house. The flashlight's beam was aimed in the direction Knotts' taillights had disappeared. He assured himself for the hundredth time this plan was going to work before giving the cord a tug.

The chainsaw roared to life.

20

By the time the flashlight's beam swooped to the chainsaw, Bobby was already rounding the corner of his house. He took a moment to observe the frantic sweeps of light across the side lawn.

"He's out there!" Wesley howled.

"I can't— I can't find him," Kerry announced.

"It's just a distraction," Decker said. "He's drawing our attention so he can strike from another side of the house."

Bobby grumbled that Decker had deduced his plans so quickly. As Pop would've told him, there was no time to sulk. This was no time to be a crybaby. He was finally going to be a trybaby. He was finally going to make Pop proud.

"*We're running out of light!*" Wesley stated.

Bobby didn't think Wesley was aware he was still shouting.

Bobby stalked around to his bedroom's side of the house where he'd left his haul from the lake. His eyes were glued to the window, making sure the beam of light didn't get pointed his way. At this range, if they opened fire on him, they weren't likely to miss.

"Toss another log in the fire," Decker directed.

"Wesley . . . what you said a minute ago . . . was it true?" Kerry asked.

Bobby had been out of earshot to have heard what Kerry was referring to. There was no time to worry about it now. He grabbed the hatchet and added the tool to the collection in his pocket, while foregoing taking the pickaxe with him. It looked too bulky for him to wield in a fight. Then he hoisted his haul over his shoulders, struggling to negotiate a firm grasp with half the fishing line spooled around his hand.

"Was Brady's plan this weekend really to . . .?" Her voice trailed off as she couldn't finish the question.

"Yes!" Wesley growled. "Now help keep an eye out for that maniac." The flashlight waved around the room as Wesley passed it to her before making his way to the hearthstone. "He's out there. Somewhere."

Bobby nearly tumbled over, balancing his haul on his shoulders. The intruders were still aiming the flashlight in the direction of the chainsaw. The sirens had cut out in the distance. They must've arrived at Mr. Harris'. There was no telling how long they would take dealing with the fire, but he had to assume they might show up at his cabin any moment.

"But . . . he *had* to know I wouldn't say yes," Kerry exclaimed, exasperated.

Through the window, Bobby could see Wesley awkwardly tossing a fresh log into the fire. His other hand clutched Pop's rifle for dear life. The fool didn't notice Bobby charging at the window.

"I'm just telling you what—"

Wesley never got to finish the thought as the shattering window cut him off.

"*He's inside!*" Kerry screamed.

Bobby dove to the ground as two shots rang out. He was sure that the thick logs of the cabin would absorb the blasts, but both sounded on target, hitting flesh.

"Did we get him?" Kerry asked.

"I think so," Decker said, smoothly. "Shine the light on the body. I don't think it's moved since it leapt through the window."

Bobby lay there in wait, not moving a muscle. The beam passed overhead, across the broken window, then dropped down. Something thudded hard against the hardwood floor. A shriek followed, hot on its tail.

"*Brady!*"

"The light, pick the light back up," Wesley pleaded frantically.

Bobby picked himself up off the ground outside, settling into a crouch. He didn't want them to spot him just yet. His deception had worked, shrinking their dwindling supply of bullets even more.

"We need to reload," Decker hissed. "Quick!"

Bobby crept to the front door, staying low to the ground. He hadn't heard Wesley move from the fireplace, and Decker had darted to retrieve the box of ammo. The beam of light flashed out through the broken window. He didn't believe Kerry was armed, having only heard two shots.

Bobby pulled the fishing line taut, then gave it a sharp tug. The cellar door it was attached to was heavier than he'd guessed. He yanked at it forcefully. Not enough to fling it open. Just enough to raise it. When he felt enough resistance at the other end of the line, he let it go.

Inside, two of them yelped as the cellar door crashed shut. Tinkling accompanied them as something skittered across the floor. Bobby charged toward the front door. He drew in the deepest breath.

They didn't barricade the front door. You saw all the furniture was still by the fire. They were so panicked they forgot to set up a blockade.

They still could've locked the door.

"Kerry!" Decker barked. "Shine the light around, see if you can find the bull—"

Decker was cut off by the crack of the front door caving in. And the screams from Kerry and Wesley.

Bobby was startled that the front door had been unlocked. It wouldn't have changed the impact of his strike. He needed to assume they had bolted the door shut, and that meant putting everything he had into his kick. He stumbled through the busted door, planting his bad knee hard on the ground in the effort to regain his footing, aggravating it worse.

He counted himself lucky he already had his hammer drawn. Decker stood there, steadfast as ever, almost as if he'd been waiting for Bobby's arrival.

He swung wildly at Decker's head, hard enough to split it open. The blow would've been vicious, but Bobby believed he'd survive. He just needed to incapacitate him quickly. Wesley was already scurrying from the corner to put as much distance between himself and Bobby. Kerry stood there, frozen in terror, shining the light in Bobby's eyes.

The light wasn't blinding, but it was enough to alter his aim. Decker deftly ducked under the swing without a single hair being touched. The hammer struck the hearthstone with enough ferocity to send sparks flying.

Decker stepped back from his next wild swing as well, unsheathing his knife. Bobby recalled how the rest of the intruders had gasped when they'd first seen it. The magnificence of its size was truly captivating.

Bobby had to pull his head back as Decker slashed at him. He tried to deflect one of the swipes and received a gash down the back of his hand, across the slash Regina had given him earlier.

"*Find those bullets!*" Decker shouted over his shoulder.

Decker lunged blade-first at Bobby's heart. Bobby twisted out of the way in time as Decker's knife stabbed the doorframe. The blade barely shifted as Decker gave it a rough tug. Bobby seized his opportunity, swinging the hammer down with malicious intent, missing Decker again, striking the wall. The force of the impact stung his slashed hand, drawing his attention to the blood that was spilling down his forearm.

"*Wesley! There!*" Kerry shouted behind him.

Bobby snapped his neck at the two of them to see Kerry aiming her flashlight at one of the remaining bullets. Wesley fumbled to pick it up and load it into Pop's rifle. He learned instantly that taking his eyes from Decker was a mistake as the brute wrapped his arms around Bobby and drove him toward the window he'd thrown Brady through.

His back slid across broken glass and grew moist. Decker ripped one of the jagged shards still hanging from the window pane free, freeing the hand Bobby held the hammer with to do it. Bobby swung the hammer claw into Decker's thigh before Decker could drive the shard into his neck.

Decker's howl drew Kerry's light.

"*Kerry*!" Wesley barked at her, recalling the light back to him.

Bobby yanked the claw out of Decker's leg, tearing open his flesh, bringing another scream to the surface. The shard of glass fell harmlessly to Decker's side as he stumbled back toward the open front door.

"*Got it*!" Wesley exclaimed.

With Decker taken care of for the moment, Bobby focused his attention on the other two. He could easily overpower both of them, probably at once, even with the injuries he'd sustained. But thanks to the light Kerry was providing, he could see Wesley was loading the rifle. Bobby froze for a moment, realizing the flashlight Kerry was wielding would show Wesley where to aim. She still kept it trained on Wesley until he chambered the bullet, unintentionally shining a spotlight on Bobby's target for him.

Bobby withdrew the hatchet from his back pocket and hurtled it at Wesley, aiming low. The ax flashed through the beam for an instant before sticking into the floor between Wesley's legs. It had the desired effect as Wesley screeched.

And pulled the trigger in terror.

Wood splintered as Wesley's errant shot hit the busted front doorway, nearly ripping off a chunk of the wooden frame. The portion of wood seemingly defied gravity, remaining suspended in the air. Bobby could see that two nails Pop had hammered into that particular section of the timber still had their tips embedded in the cabin and were holding on for dear life.

Glancing at where Wesley's shot had gone, Bobby also saw that Decker had regained his footing. Bobby surveyed the other intruders. Wesley was on all fours, looking for another bullet to load into the rifle. Kerry was sweeping the flashlight across the floor for him. Neither appeared threatening.

Decker dodged the hammer aimed at his head, but snarled when Bobby's momentum crashed into him. He went sprawling backward, his back crashing hard against the wall around the front door and into the handle of his knife, jarring it loose from where it had been stuck in the wall. Decker instinctively reached down to pick it up, saving his life as Bobby swung his hammer at Decker's neck, striking the wall, instead.

The impact of striking the thick log radiated up Bobby's arm. His grip of the hammer's handle had been weakening since Decker had cut him open, but he'd managed to ignore it while he focused all his attention on his enemy. The pain captured all his focus now, and the hammer slipped harmlessly from his hand as he tried to tourniquet the agony at the wrist with his left hand.

Decker found the knife's handle, but before he could wrap his fingers around it, Bobby grabbed his head with his good hand and slammed it back against the wall. The bang of Decker's skull meeting the wood drew the attention of the flashlight.

Both Decker's hands flew to Bobby's skull, trying to tear it off his head. Bobby grabbed the side of Decker's head with his damaged hand as best he could, grasping a clump of sweaty hair and a piece of ear, and drove the man's head back against the unforgiving wall. After the third time, Bobby noticed a spot of dampness where he'd been bashing Decker's skull against it.

The beam of light illuminating them dropped. Behind him, the flashlight clattered to the floor. He imagined Kerry had fainted at seeing Decker getting pummeled. He expected Decker would lose consciousness in a few seconds, leaving him with only Wesley to deal with. As long as the twerp hadn't reloaded Pop's rifle, Bobby expected he'd have all three subdued in minutes.

"Kerry!" Wesley rasped. "What're you doing? Help me move the couch. There're two rounds underneath it."

Bobby paused from slamming Decker's head against the wall a final time. Wesley's words didn't sound like a reaction to someone who was passed out.

He didn't have time to turn to see the impact, or brace himself for it. Kerry propelled herself into his back, rocking his entire body. The pain that he'd been able to ignore from his ribs, knee, shoulder, and back while he'd engaged Decker in combat began radiating in full force. He doubled over to protect his ribs from more damage, and his sore knee buckled under him. The sudden movement wreaked havoc on his shoulder, and the surrounding muscles tightened in response. He felt old and worn out.

Should've known better than to think she'd fainted. She's a trybaby, through and through.

You got bigger problems.

There was a spark in Decker's eyes after seeing Kerry jump in to save him. He needed the wall to prop himself back to his feet, but he looked more invigorated by the second.

Bobby needed to put him down fast.

Kerry rained fists on his back. He involuntarily flinched when she struck his bruised shoulder, leading her to hone all her pounding to that one spot. Bobby blindly threw an elbow behind him. He heard a gasp as he connected, and caught sight of her falling through the open door. She grabbed at the doorway to halt her drop, seizing the broken piece of wood held by the two nails and yanking it from the frame.

All seemed lost when Bobby felt Decker's hands around his throat. The firm grip yanked him close, but when it did, Bobby could see the profuse rate his nemesis was panting and sweating. Bobby felt a surge of adrenaline course through his veins as he realized his enemy was struggling, too.

Bobby head-butted his foe square in the nose. Decker's face grew wet with blood, though Bobby suspected most of it was from his own face. It didn't matter. The blow had rattled Decker enough to loosen his grip from Bobby's neck. He clutched Decker's head, firmly grasping one side of Decker's face with his left hand, settling for pinning his bad hand against the other side of Decker's face, and prepared to crack his skull open like an egg.

He howled as his hands slipped from Decker's crown to the back of his leg. Bobby twisted to see Kerry had swung the debris she had ripped from the doorway into his leg, impaling his right calf with the two nails.

His scream was interrupted with a haymaker from Decker. The tear in his chin from his scrum with Brady split open again. His blood splashed down his neck as he tumbled backward against the fireplace, knocking over the metal container that held the poker, sweeper, and a metal pan to collect the ash.

"*Got them!*" Wesley announced from across the room.

Behind him, the log Wesley had tossed into the fireplace moments before Bobby broke into his own house finally settled into the flames. The room lit up in an orange glow as Kerry burst through the door and Decker stooped down to retrieve his knife. As the two advanced on him, the shadows they cast looked as wicked as their owners. All they had to do was hold him down until Wesley loaded Pop's rifle and pulled the trigger, but their eyes told the story they'd torture him until Wesley was ready.

Bobby flailed his good hand blindly for something to defend himself with, while his right tried to retrieve the screwdriver from his pocket. It was cramping into a claw, making it nearly impossible to grip the tool. His left hand found the handle of the metal pan. He shoved it into the fireplace, scooping out some of the embers, and flung it at his attackers.

Three hit Kerry across the face. She shrieked as she retreated, batting her face, desperate to extinguish the scorching debris. One sailed toward Wesley, who yelped. A moment later, something small clattered across the floor. Bobby was sure Wesley had dropped the bullets. The clattering continued, splitting into two distinct patterns. One grew faint as it disappeared down the basement steps. The other thumped against wood, and morphed into a roll across the floor.

Decker's dodge of Bobby's hot ash came at a price as his torn knee faltered and gave out on him. He dove blade-first at Bobby's neck, missing high and slicing across his cheek and nose.

Bobby raised both hands defensively. With the thug on top of him, it was the only option that remained. Decker grabbed Bobby's damaged hand to move it out of the way, ready to plunge the knife into Bobby's jugular. He couldn't get a firm grasp, as Bobby's sliced hand had grown slippery. His grip slipped off the wound, peeling back the skin around Bobby's cut in the process. Bobby seethed as he intercepted Decker's knife hand.

Decker lost his balance in his attempt to impale Bobby. Bobby recognized Decker's effort to regain his dominant position, and began to writhe wildly on the ground, trying to buck Decker off him. The two began to wrestle across the floor in an effort to pin each other. The furniture they crashed into merely altered their course as they rolled through the living room. He squealed each time the back of his leg struck the floor, pounding the two nails deeper into his calf.

"*Wesley!*" Kerry called out. To Bobby, she sounded like she was standing near Pop's rifle collection. "*Help Decker out! Club that maniac with the gun!*"

Bobby realized he and Decker had tussled across the room into the kitchen. He braced himself for

Wesley's blows, not sure he could withstand an attack from both at once.

He heard the scampering across the floor, but instead of approaching, Wesley had shuffled away from the fight.

"*Hang on!*" Wesley cried. "Almost got the shot loaded."

The back of Decker's head struck one of the kitchen table legs. He immediately let go of Bobby to soothe his cranium. Bobby noticed Decker had lost his knife along the way, and took the opportunity to pry the nails from his leg. He'd just removed them when strong hands closed on his throat, yanking him to his feet.

He had no time to be surprised that Decker had sprung to his feet so quickly. The tough hands squeezed his windpipe, choking the life out of him. Bobby could feel his eyes redden, and peered into Decker's, searching for mercy. What he saw told him Decker intended to release him only when his body went limp and would never stir again.

"Come on, get in there," Wesley grumbled behind Decker, fumbling to load the round into the chamber.

Bobby knew he'd either be strangled to death or his head would be blown off if he didn't do something fast. He reached into his pocket for the screwdriver, but his bloody hand had tightened into a fist he couldn't uncurl. Bobby extended his left hand awkwardly across his body to the opposite pocket to extract the tool.

Decker's grip tightened around his neck. Bobby gasped for air to no avail. He chopped his sliced hand down on Decker's wrists, getting the worst of it. It felt like he'd struck rock. The screwdriver refused to be summoned from his pocket.

Decker stared down at him with murderous intent. Bobby couldn't bear the diabolical look anymore. Arms weakening by the second, he flailed his cut hand toward Decker's face, poking him in the eye. Decker snarled, but Bobby paid no attention. His lungs had got the taste of fresh air as Decker's grasp faltered slightly. He drove his hand into Decker's socket. Bobby couldn't muster the force to gouge his eye out, but it was enough to drive the brute off him, sending him stumbling backward over the table.

The unmistakable sound of a round being loaded into a chamber cut through the air. Bobby ripped the screwdriver from his pocket as he turned to see Wesley aiming the rifle. He still needed to catch his breath, but knew he'd only have one try at this.

"Die, you—"

Bobby lunged at the rifle, stabbing the screwdriver down its barrel, hoping to jam the path. If he missed, he was essentially lining up Wesley's shot for him.

"*Wesley!*" Kerry screamed from the corner of the living room. It was clear she'd seen what Bobby had done. "*Don't pull—!*"

"*MOTHERFU—!*"

Wesley pulled the trigger, and the rifle instantly erupted as the round struck the screwdriver lodged in the barrel. With nowhere else to go, the explosion shot back toward Wesley. The stock of the rifle flew backward, ricocheting off the wall. Wesley had been resting his cheek against it as he fired. The blast ripped off that half of his face.

Wesley's hands dropped what was left of the firearm to clutch at what remained of his face. When he screamed, it sounded strange and distorted. Bobby was pretty sure his vocal cords had been ripped to shreds by the detonation.

The kitchen table slammed into Bobby's hip when Wesley crashed into it. With half his face missing, Wesley had begun running around the kitchen the same way Regina had. His own good eye was shut. The one caught in the blast no longer had an eyelid, but Bobby doubted Wesley could see through it anymore. The throaty shrieks trailed the racing body through the house, even when Wesley raced through the open cellar door, and tumbled down the steps. By the third sickening thud, the wails cut off permanently.

A battle cry came from deep within Kerry as she leapt at Bobby. Bobby felt his nose get readjusted as she swung the stock of another of Pop's rifles at him. A fresh flow of blood spilled over his mouth as he was knocked back. He pieced together that after she'd extinguished the embers from her face, Kerry was standing in front of Pop's gun case. She hadn't needed it to be loaded to use it as a weapon.

Kerry hammered the stock down on the wrist of his good hand. Bobby couldn't afford to have that go useless as well, not with two intruders still fighting. He kicked out with his left leg, ignoring the jolt to his swollen knee, because the gored calf of his right leg wasn't allowing that range in motion. His leg stiffened, but it got the job done, planting a kick in Kerry's diaphragm. She was knocked back, screeched, and dropped the rifle. When Bobby drew near her, he saw the edge of the hatchet he'd thrown at Wesley was sticking out between two of her toes.

A fist pummeled his cheek, nearly knocking him down the cellar steps. Decker had managed to get to his feet again, though the effort looked laborious. He was panting heavily, swaying back and forth, but he still had some fight in him.

Bobby slipped Decker's next punch, weaving to his left, back into the living room, but the next one caught him in the eye. He felt it swelling shut as Decker connected with his jaw. Bobby stumbled backward, continuing to backpedal as Decker hobbled after him. Decker was on him as soon as his back collided with the window, cutting off his escape.

Decker heaved himself into Bobby, pinning him up against the glass that cracked, but didn't break. Bobby was sure his ribs finally cracked when Decker landed a shot to his midsection, doubling him over for good. Hunched over, Bobby was able to duck Decker's next swing, which connected with the glass pane, adding more cracks to it. Decker's next uppercut found Bobby's head, rocking it back, lifting him off the ground and into the window, finally shattering it. If the shards of glass slashed at his back, he didn't notice. He couldn't focus on one source of pain anymore.

Bobby cried as Decker grabbed his skull from both sides and started to squeeze. Decker drove Bobby's head toward the splintered glass still stuck in the window frame. His grip was sloppy, and his thumb slid into Bobby's mouth. With no weapons left, Bobby clamped down on the digit.

Decker's shrieks reinvigorated Bobby to keep fighting. He hooked his damaged claw of a hand around the back of Decker's neck and yanked him toward the glass, exchanging positions with his opponent. He knew the shards had stabbed into Decker's gut even before Decker roared.

The familiar battle cry sounded behind him. He knew he should've expected Kerry to remain in the fight. Bobby turned to see her limping as fast she could, brandishing the bloody hatchet. He dove backward, grimacing each time he had to plant his bad knee and gored calf. His bloody hand was still snagged around Decker's neck, halting his escape. The image of Kerry cleaving through it, leaving him with a stump, flashed through his mind. He tugged with everything he had left, pulling his claw free from around Decker's neck, dragging Decker across the mountain range of shards in the process.

Decker's cries weakened as the glass cut through him. By the time Kerry hacked into his back with the hatchet, all he could manage was a faint gasp.

"Deck . . . Decker?" Kerry asked timidly, slowly backing away from what she'd done.

Decker slowly pried himself from the line of glass that had impaled him. He didn't even seem to notice the blade stuck in his shoulder. He turned to face them, shuffling slowly, both hands pressed to his damp shirt. By the time he'd fully rotated, his eyes were vacant, and rolled to the top of his eye sockets. His bloody hands dropped to his sides. Bobby saw they'd been the only thing keeping his insides inside. When he'd dragged Decker across the glass, he'd ripped the man's stomach open. He and Kerry watched in horror as Decker collapsed onto the mound of guts that had spilled out of him.

Headlights swept across the room, highlighting the last intruder Bobby had to deal with. He hadn't meant for Decker to die, but he didn't believe he'd dealt the deathblow. Bobby regretted that Decker was dead, but was relieved that only Kerry remained. As far as he knew, Wesley still lay unconscious in the cellar.

Hunchbacked and hobbling, he advanced on her. Her charge with the hatchet had been slow going, limping the entire way. Bobby believed he could overpower her in seconds.

He overshot his first approach as she evaded his grasp. Bobby turned back to her, reaching for her neck with his good hand. He realized his mistake too late.

The hatchet hadn't been the only weapon Kerry had armed herself with. She had also scooped up Decker's huge blade before getting to her feet and making her charge. As he tried to seize her, she unsheathed it from her belt, stabbing through the palm of his hand.

Kerry's howl drowned out his own as she drove him back, steering him toward the hearthstone. The log had been nearly consumed, and the blaze had begun to die down, but it was strong enough to cook him if she could guide him into the flames.

The intensity in her eyes was fiercer than anything he'd seen in Decker's. He questioned whether he shouldn't have focused his attention on her this whole time. Decker had appeared the more imposing threat, but she was summoning a fury Decker had never matched.

His back slammed into the hearthstone, rocking his body. There was no last wave of adrenaline to call upon. The fight was oozing out of the hand she had pierced. Bobby's legs wobbled, threatening to give out on him.

He knew he was done for if he didn't act quickly. But even if he had one last tool on him he could use as a weapon, he didn't have a working hand to hold it. There was only one thing he could think to do.

Kerry was caught off guard when he snapped his head toward her. By the time she realized his intentions, it was too late.

Bobby clamped his teeth down hard on her neck. Her screams were swallowed up in the throat he was squeezing shut. He shook his head back and forth, copying nature videos he'd seen when predators held prey in their jaws. When he released her, he spit out a chunk of her flesh.

Her hands flew from the hilt of the knife to her neck. She crumpled to the ground. A waterfall of blood had already gushed down her shirt.

Bloody teeth bared, he grabbed hold of the knife as best he could with his claw of a hand, and slid it as delicately as he could out of the middle of his palm. Bobby dropped to one knee before he'd freed it from his flesh.

He rushed to stagger to his feet, then saw there was no need. Kerry had stopped thrashing from the tear across her neck, but wasn't close to regaining her feet. When she saw him rise, she backpedaled from him, stopping when she bumped into Brady's corpse. She turned to see what was obstructing her path, letting out a gurgled scream.

More cradling the knife in the crook of his hand than holding it, Bobby shambled toward her. Bobby couldn't lift his legs, merely sliding them across the floor, but it didn't matter. He had her now, and all he had left to do was figure out a way to restrain her until he could call the state police. His original plan had been to bind them all with fishing line, but he wasn't sure how he was going to do that now with two damaged hands.

"*Leave us alone!*" Kerry shrieked, her voice scratchy from the wound to her neck. "*We just wanted a relaxing vacation after graduating college!*"

A gun went off from the front door behind him, and he felt the bullet bite into his bruised shoulder. A moment later, he was lying face down in a pool of his own blood.

21

"*Jesus Christ, Bobby!*" the familiar voice screamed at him. "*What the hell have you done?*"

Bobby didn't dare writhe away the pain, fearing every movement would only bring agony. Through his watery eyes, he caught a glimpse of his reflection in a shard of glass balanced against the wall. He didn't even recognize the bloody, haggard monster staring back at him.

"He attacked us, Sher—"

"I defengdhehd mythelf," Bobby roared over Kerry. "Pleathe don't khill me. I got attaghed by him."

He unconsciously pointed at Brady with the hand Kerry had pierced with the knife, noting that the pain wasn't as bad as he thought. Bobby started to test out how much mobility the rest of his limbs had when he heard Knotts' footsteps close in on him.

"Looks like you got the better of it," Knotts observed dryly to Bobby.

"Oh, Brady," Kerry wept as she scooted over to Brady's corpse. She studied it with curiosity for a moment, then fished through his pockets.

"Miss, I'm sorry, but you can't touch the body. I'm going to need to preserve it until we can deter—"

Kerry gasped. Tears poured down her face. One hand shot to her mouth to block another scream. The other held a diamond ring.

"Oh god, Brady," she said, sniffling. "They weren't lying about your big plans. You really were going to . . . and I wouldn't have . . . ." She broke down in tears before she could finish her sentence.

"You all right, darlin'?" Knotts asked. "I woulda been here sooner—"

I *knew* it! Knotts is involved in this plot.

He's checking to make sure his minions are okay.

"—when I heard a gun go off from the neighbor's house, but me and the boys from the fire department couldn't tell for certain if it was a firearm or a firecracker. When we heard a single blast minutes later, I decided to go check it out."

"I'm fine!" she insisted, scrubbing moisture from her cheeks. "Check them. Decker's over there," she said, pointing across the room, "and Wesley fell down the stairs."

Heavy boots stepped over Bobby, making their way to the cellar door. Bobby glanced up to see Knotts kept his gun on him. The sheriff aimed his flashlight down into the cellar.

"He's gone, darlin'," Knotts reported. "Necks ain't supposed to twist that way."

"*I wath defenghding mythelf!*" Bobby shouted, making Kerry wince.

He wasn't sure why he was bothering pleading his case. This was ideal for Knotts, catching him with multiple victims in his house. Knotts had more than enough evidence to haul him away and finally search the premises. What was more, the victims were the hoodlums involved in Knotts' plot to rob the place. Now the sheriff not only didn't need to divvy out their cut, if Kerry demanded a larger share of the haul by threatening to expose the sheriff's involvement, no one was left to verify her story.

Knotts sauntered back over to him, keeping his gun pointed at Bobby's forehead. Bobby was battered all over, but even with a bullet hole in him, he knew he could still move. The only problem was he was certain Knotts would put another one in him if he stirred.

"Cheryl," Knotts said into his walkie-talkie, "send everybody. I don't care how much they bitch about the hour. We . . . got a situation here. Multiple casualties."

Wait. He's . . . calling it in.

They're all *in on it. Knotts promised all his deputies a cut.*

No. No, something's not right.

"*Oh, lord.*" The dispatcher wept softly on the other end. "*More people were burned alive in—?*"

"No," Knotts cut her off. "I'm not there anymore. I'm next door. There's . . . it's a mess over here. I need everyone."

"Oh, Brady," Kerry continued to weep. "You *had* to know my answer. Even your plans to ask me . . . they were all about *you.* You chose this cabin and invited your friends because it reminded you of all the times you and Decker took these camping trips. None of this would've hap— They'd all still be— We wouldn't've come here if you weren't going to ask."

Knotts kept his gun trained on Bobby as he went to inspect Decker's body. Bobby eyed him intently, only shifting on the floor to see how much he could move when the sheriff looked away. He had more mobility than he would've thought. Something poked his belly, and he realized he was lying on top of Decker's knife. Bobby also understood that Knotts didn't know about the blade.

"*The neighbor's?*" Cheryl squawked through the radio. "*You're at that Dinwill's place?*"

See? See? She called you a dimwit.

Stop. You know that's not what she said.

"Yes," Knotts growled, trudging back to Bobby. "Now rouse everyone, hear me?"

Knotts' boots stopped inches in front of Bobby's face. The sheriff was well within arm's reach, and if Bobby wanted to, he could easily slash Knotts' leg with the knife. He remained motionless. He was still facing the floor, but knew the barrel was pointed at the back of his head.

He didn't tell her you were alive. He could still put you down.

But why wait? Why not do it immediately? And if the intruders were working for him, why call it in at all? Something doesn't add up.

"What a mess," Knotts commented absently. "What the hell have you done, boy? You been taking your meds?" He paused thoughtfully, then shot out a question like it'd just hit him. "Did you burn down the Harris place, too?"

"No! *They* diddit when they attagged me!" Bobby protested.

"They attacked you here. They attacked you there. Damn, son, where *didn't* they at—"

"Wait!" Kerry interjected. "*That* was the Harris place?" Bobby was still staring at the bloodstained floorboards, but he got the sense Knotts nodded. "Oh, god," she gasped. "We went to the wrong house!"

Her declaration sent Bobby's mind racing until he felt dizzy. It couldn't have all been one giant misunderstanding. They were mobsters from Chicago! He kept insisting it as fact, yet simultaneously played devil's advocate to everything he thought he knew.

Knotts sounded just as befuddled. "Oh, dang it. That's right, it *was* Harris who told me he was planning on renting his cabin out for the holidays. Makes more sense that someone with his entrepreneurial mindset would rent his place out." His voice grew sheepish. "When I was here earlier, I coulda sworn you guys were supposed to be at the Harris place, but he'd told me about it weeks ago at that point, and I figured you guys had known where to go."

That's the Knotts I remember, bumbling the details again.

He's lying! She and him are changing their stories on the fly.

But Mr. Harris did leave for the weekend. I talked to him as he was driving away. Knotts blundered another detail, is all. If he forgot Mr. Harris told him he was renting out his cabin, Knotts could've forgotten who'd told him was going to be gone this weekend.

He could've hired the goons to come down from Chicago because he thought it was you who'd told him the house would be vacant.

No, that doesn't add up. If Knotts thought I was the one renting my house, he wouldn't have hired anyone to rob the place because of the renters who'd be staying here.

Okay, Knotts fudged a detail again. That doesn't explain how the intruders made the same mistake.

Pop built Mr. Harris' house to look like our own. I saw Mr. Harris even kept his spare key in the same spot.

But . . . they-they were talking about big plans. And Momma's ring.

The ring Kerry pulled out of his pocket has a rock bigger than anything Pop would've ever bought.

But they . . . I . . . Brady beat me.

Brady seemed ready to fight anybody.

You . . . I . . . I. . . .

I need my meds.

"*Russell is on his way, Sheriff,*" Cheryl's voice squawked over the radio. "*I'm giving Cooper a ring now.*"

"Thank you, Cheryl," Knotts said into his walkie-talkie. "Darlin', I need you to step away from the body. I'm sorry this happened to you, but my boys'll need to process the scene. Shouldn't take too long. Seems pretty cut and dried. I get the sense Bobby here hasn't been keeping up with his prescription."

Knotts' statement brought Bobby's battle with his inner demon to a ceasefire. He realized he was squeezing the hilt of Decker's knife hard enough to choke the life out of it.

"He's fine when he's on 'em—"

They're going to blame this all on you.

Stop. I'm not listening to you anymore. Look at what I've done because of you.

"—keeps him focused—"

They're going to lock you up.

Shut up!

"—on reality—"

Five dead. And arson. They're going to fry you for this.

Oh, god! What'm I gonna do?

"—though I've never seen it this bad when he's been off them."

Kerry nodded, but struggled to rise.

"Here, let me help you," Knotts offered, taking a step toward her.

You know what you've got to do. Do it. Do it now!

Bobby rolled to his side, freeing the knife buried under him. With a grotesque snarl, he swung the knife into Knotts' leg, aiming above the thick boot Knotts wore. Decker's blade sliced through Knotts' muscles like they were butter.

Knotts wailed, releasing his gun, which clattered to the floor, before toppling to the ground. Kerry's terror drowned out Knotts' agony. Bobby's claw of a hand couldn't maintain its grip on the hilt as he forced himself to rise to his feet. A cool breeze from the broken window stung his body everywhere it had been split open from the brawl.

The sheriff writhed in torment, clutching at his gored leg. Satisfied that he was dealt with, Bobby turned his attention to the trybaby. She'd shown time and again the amount of fight she had in her, and Bobby had the sense that well hadn't run dry.

She didn't disappoint him.

Kerry plucked Knotts' gun from the floor and fired it wildly at his head. Bobby ducked as the first four shots sailed high. She noticed as well, lowering her aim before the chamber emptied.

Bobby's head rocked to the side as the last shot hit his temple. He barreled toward the broken window and spilled out of the house. Everything went dark before he hit the ground.

22

"Sheriff, are you all right?" Kerry asked as she tossed another log into the fire. Even though the maniac was gone, she wasn't certain he was dead, and the room had grown too dark for her liking.

"I'll be fine," Knotts grimaced. "Do me a favor, darlin', and help me up."

Kerry eyed the broken window the psycho had disappeared from, as she hobbled to the sheriff. She found she did most of the work lifting him to his feet, and feared her split foot would give out before he found his footing.

Both their heads twisted to the snap of a branch coming from outside the broken window. The guttural groan confirmed the monster wasn't dead.

Knotts snapped his fingers. "My gun. Give it here." He snapped again impatiently. "It needs reloading."

Kerry tried to remember how many shots she'd fired. All she could recall was pulling the trigger until bullets stopped flying out. Empty chambers would do them no good if he came back.

She relinquished the firearm to him, and he deftly inserted a fresh clip with a full magazine. Leaning on each other, they shambled to the window. The maniac wasn't lying outside, gasping his last breath. A cursory scan with Knotts' flashlight revealed the fiend had crawled down the hill to the lake, into a waiting rowboat.

"Don't worry, he's badly injured," Knotts said as they watched the monster crawl into the boat. "He won't get far."

The psycho pushed off from the shore, beyond the reach of Knotts' flashlight, disappearing into the darkness. Kerry could feel the sheriff stiffen in her grasp, and had no doubt he felt her tense up as well.

"We'll catch him," he said, although she wasn't sure if the reassurance was for her benefit, or his.

Kerry didn't share his confidence.

Enjoyed Lock the Doors?

Thanks for tagging along with the reclusive Bobby Dinwill. If you enjoyed the mayhem, please leave a review as it helps other readers discover the story.

Author's Note

More books by Damian Myron

Thanks for tagging along with the reclusive Bobby Dinwill. Be sure to read about the thrilling pursuit of Rob Moore in Damian's debut novel, *Dig Down*. More books by Damian Myron will be coming soon. Sign up for the Reader's List on the homepage of damianmyronwrites.com to be notified of future books.

*Still craving more **Lock the Doors?***

Visit the blog page of damianmyronwrites.com for weekly serials set in the *Dig Down* universe, and see what some of the other characters were up to before getting mixed up with Rob.

About the Author

Damian Myron was educated at Siena College. He lives in New York where he spends most of his time dreaming of other worlds.

Acknowledgments

I'd like to offer a special thanks to those whose contributions helped me realize my vision for this book. My editor, Dorrie O'Brien, who challenged me with round after round of revisions to bring this story to life. And Natasha Mackenzie, for designing an eye catching book cover that fit in both the worlds of thriller and horror.